STONE ARCH BOOKS
a capstone imprint

THE BATMAN STRIKES!

▼▼ STONE ARCH BOOKS™

Published in 2014
A Capstone Imprint
1710 Roe Crest Drive
North Mankato, MN 56003
www.capstonepub.com

Originally published by DC Comics in the U.S. in
single magazine form as The Batman Strikes! #1.
Copyright © 2014 DC Comics. All Rights Reserved.

DC Comics
1700 Broadway, New York, NY 10019
A Warner Bros. Entertainment Company

Printed in China by Nordica.
1013/CA21301918
092013 007744NORD514

Cataloging-in-Publication Data is available at the
Library of Congress website:
ISBN: 978-1-4342-6483-1 (library binding)

Summary: In this story starring a young Batman
who is new to crime-fighting, the Penguin pulls
a heist that could reveal Bruce Wayne's secret
identity and destroy vast portions of Gotham City!

STONE ARCH BOOKS
Ashley C. Andersen Zantop *Publisher*
Michael Dahl *Editorial Director*
Sean Tulien *Editor*
Heather Kindseth *Creative Director*
Bob Lentz *Designer*
Kathy McColley *Production Specialist*

DC COMICS
Joan Hilty & Harvey Richards *Original U.S. Editors*
Jeff Matsuda & Dave McCaig *Cover Artists*

IN THE CLUTCHES OF THE PENGUIN!

BILL MATHENY ....WRITER
CHRISTOPHER JONES ....PENCILLER
TERRY BEATTY...INKER
HEROIC AGE ....COLORIST
PAT BROSSEAU ....LETTERER

BATMAN CREATED BY
BOB KANE

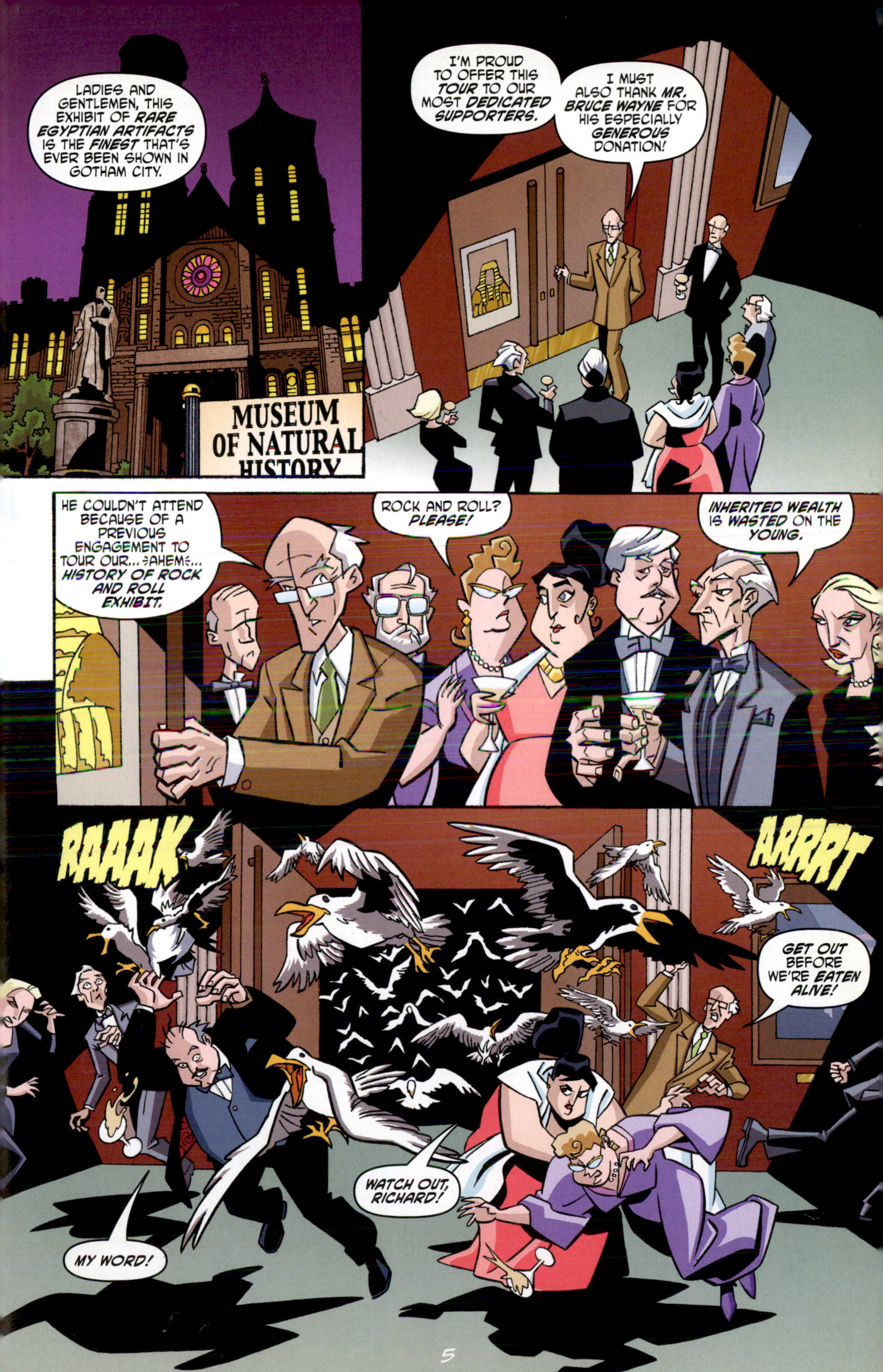

LADIES AND GENTLEMEN, THIS EXHIBIT OF RARE EGYPTIAN ARTIFACTS IS THE FINEST THAT'S EVER BEEN SHOWN IN GOTHAM CITY.
MUSEUM OF NATURAL HISTORY
I'M PROUD TO OFFER THIS TOUR TO OUR MOST DEDICATED SUPPORTERS.
I MUST ALSO THANK MR. BRUCE WAYNE FOR HIS ESPECIALLY GENEROUS DONATION!
HE COULDN'T ATTEND BECAUSE OF A PREVIOUS ENGAGEMENT TO TOUR OUR... AHEM... HISTORY OF ROCK AND ROLL EXHIBIT.
ROCK AND ROLL? PLEASE!
INHERITED WEALTH IS WASTED ON THE YOUNG.
RAAAK
ARRRT
GET OUT BEFORE WE'RE EATEN ALIVE!
WATCH OUT, RICHARD!
MY WORD!

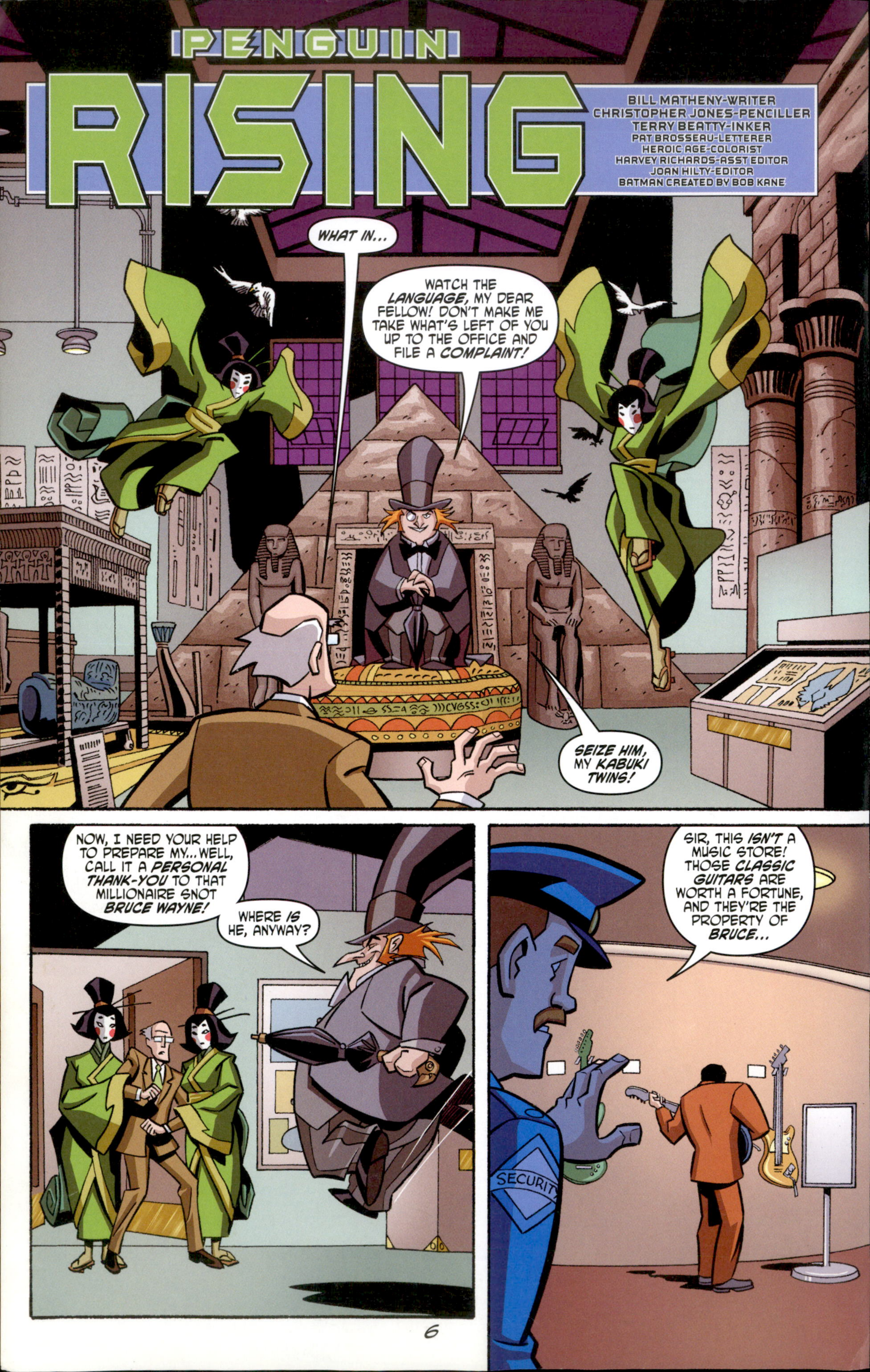
PENGUIN
RISING
BILL MATHENY-WRITER
CHRISTOPHER JONES-PENCILLER
TERRY BEATTY-INKER
PAT BROSSEAU-LETTERER
HEROIC AGE-COLORIST
HARVEY RICHARDS-ASST EDITOR
JOAN HILTY-EDITOR
BATMAN CREATED BY BOB KANE
WHAT IN...
WATCH THE LANGUAGE, MY DEAR FELLOW! DON'T MAKE ME TAKE WHAT'S LEFT OF YOU UP TO THE OFFICE AND FILE A COMPLAINT!
SEIZE HIM, MY KABUKI TWINS!
NOW, I NEED YOUR HELP TO PREPARE MY...WELL, CALL IT A PERSONAL THANK-YOU TO THAT MILLIONAIRE SNOT BRUCE WAYNE!
WHERE IS HE, ANYWAY?
SIR, THIS ISN'T A MUSIC STORE! THOSE CLASSIC GUITARS ARE WORTH A FORTUNE, AND THEY'RE THE PROPERTY OF BRUCE...
SECURITY

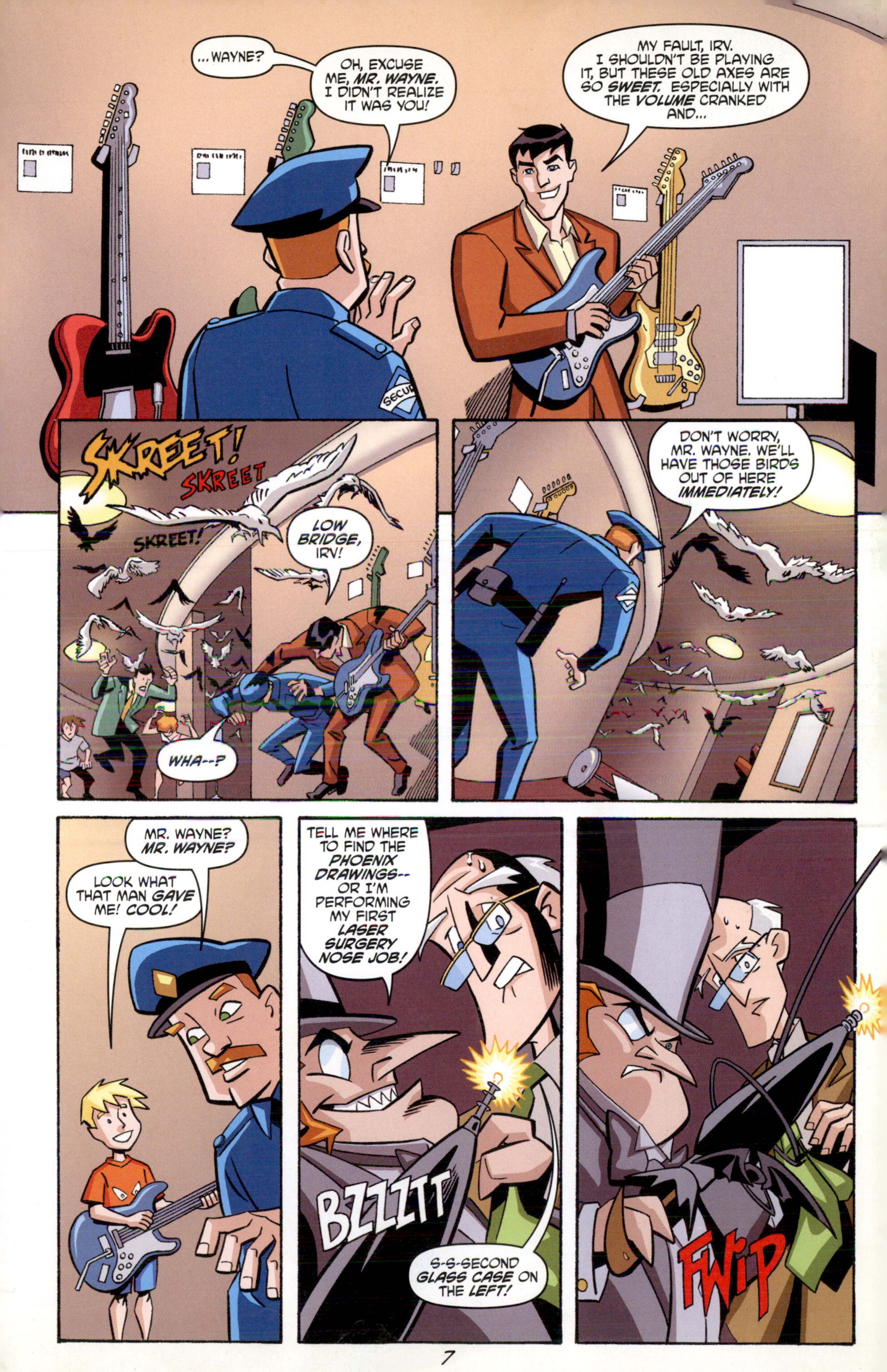
...WAYNE?
OH, EXCUSE ME, MR. WAYNE. I DIDN'T REALIZE IT WAS YOU!
MY FAULT, IRV. I SHOULDN'T BE PLAYING IT, BUT THESE OLD AXES ARE SO SWEET. ESPECIALLY WITH THE VOLUME CRANKED AND...
SKREET!
SKREET
SKREET!
LOW BRIDGE, IRV!
WHA--?
DON'T WORRY, MR. WAYNE. WE'LL HAVE THOSE BIRDS OUT OF HERE IMMEDIATELY!
MR. WAYNE? MR. WAYNE?
LOOK WHAT THAT MAN GAVE ME! COOL!
TELL ME WHERE TO FIND THE PHOENIX DRAWINGS-- OR I'M PERFORMING MY FIRST LASER SURGERY NOSE JOB!
BZZZTT
S-S-SECOND GLASS CASE ON THE LEFT!
FWIP

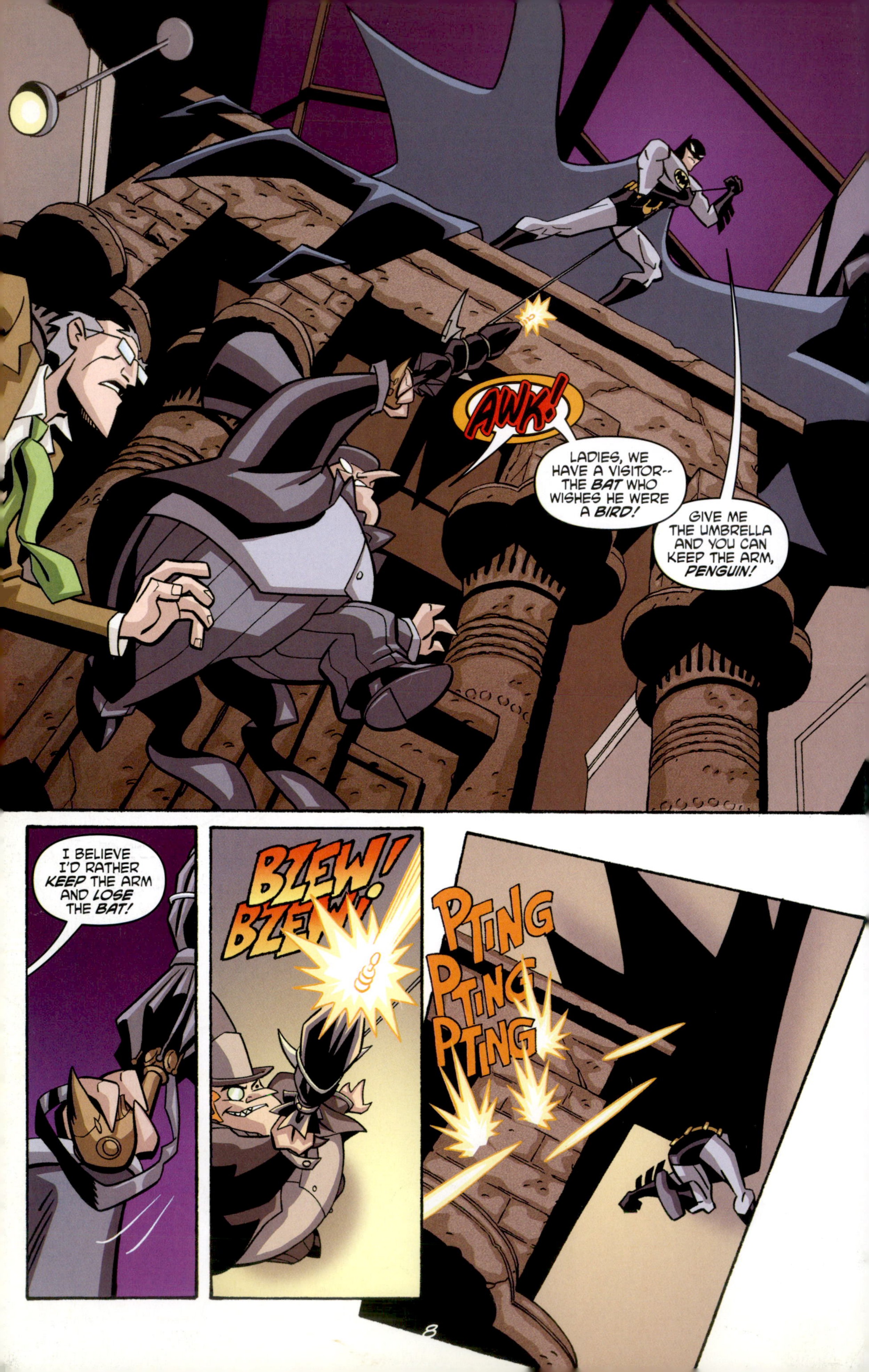
AWK!
LADIES, WE HAVE A VISITOR-- THE BAT WHO WISHES HE WERE A BIRD!
GIVE ME THE UMBRELLA AND YOU CAN KEEP THE ARM, PENGUIN!
I BELIEVE I'D RATHER KEEP THE ARM AND LOSE THE BAT!
BZEW! BZEW!
PTING PTING PTING

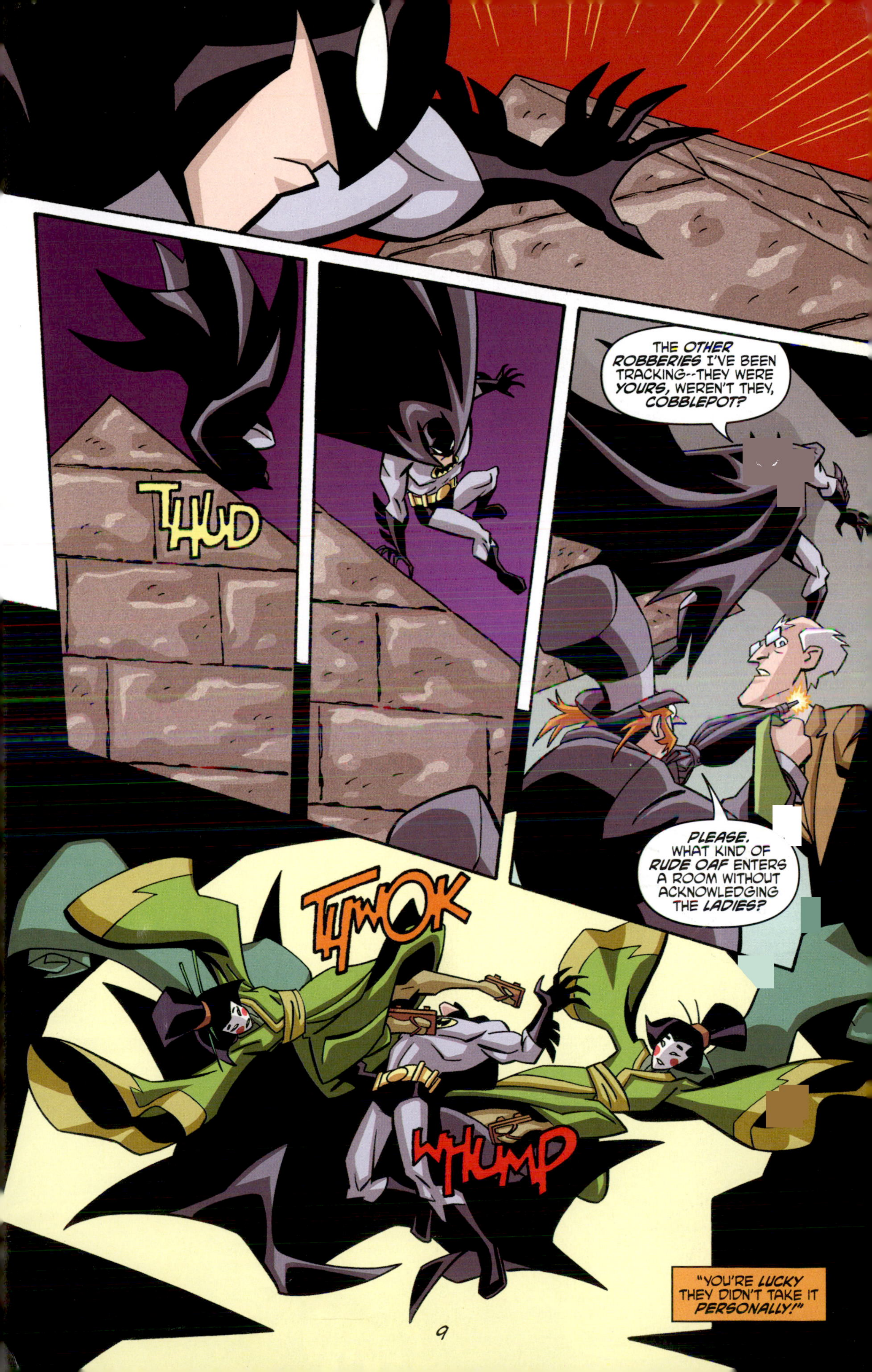
THUD
THE OTHER ROBBERIES I'VE BEEN TRACKING--THEY WERE YOURS, WEREN'T THEY, COBBLEPOT?
PLEASE. WHAT KIND OF RUDE OAF ENTERS A ROOM WITHOUT ACKNOWLEDGING THE LADIES?
THWOK
WHUMP
"YOU'RE LUCKY THEY DIDN'T TAKE IT PERSONALLY!"

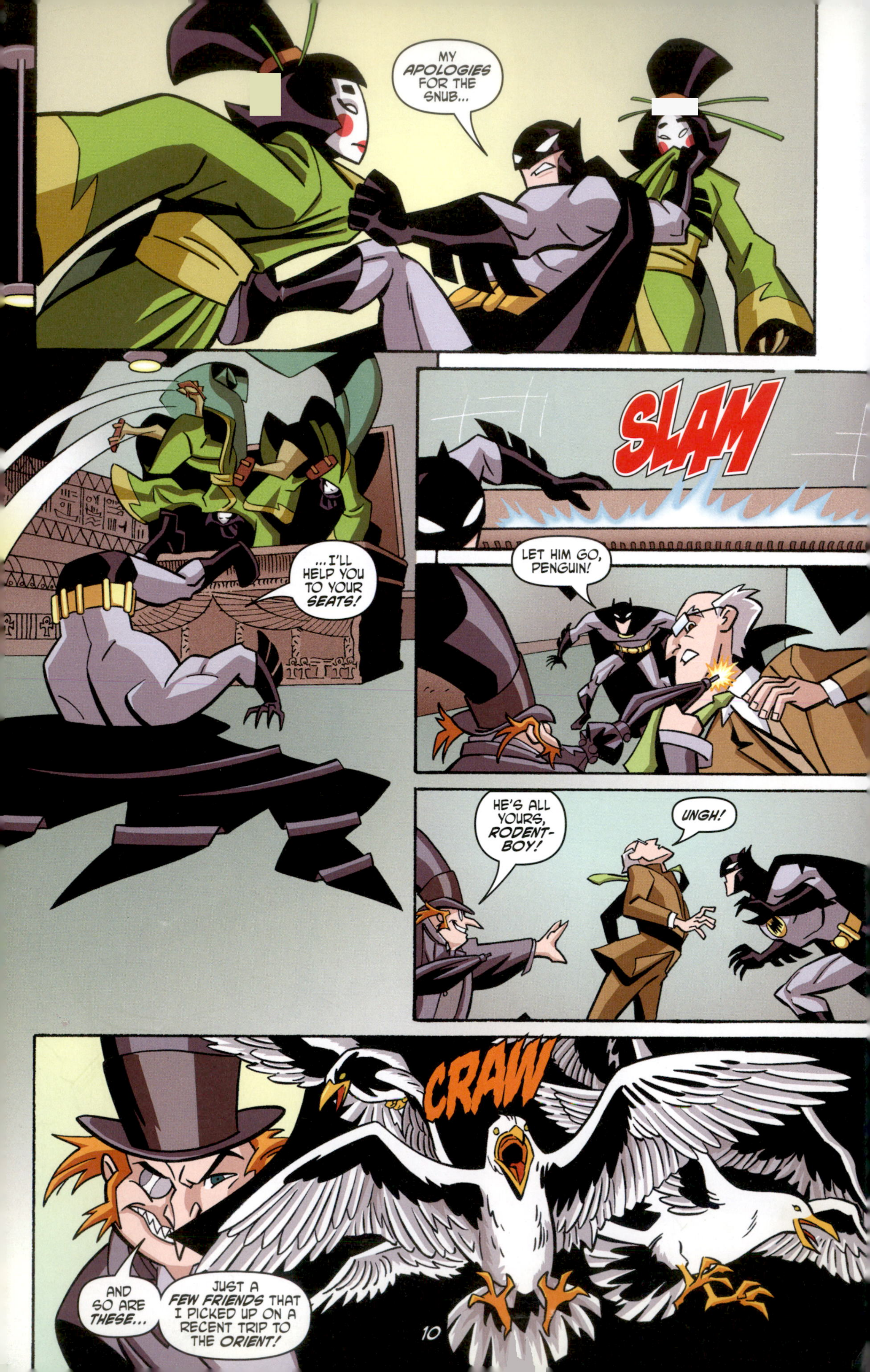

MY APOLOGIES FOR THE SNUB...
...I'LL HELP YOU TO YOUR SEATS!
SLAM
LET HIM GO, PENGUIN!
HE'S ALL YOURS, RODENT-BOY!
UNGH!
CRAW
AND SO ARE THESE...
JUST A FEW FRIENDS THAT I PICKED UP ON A RECENT TRIP TO THE ORIENT!

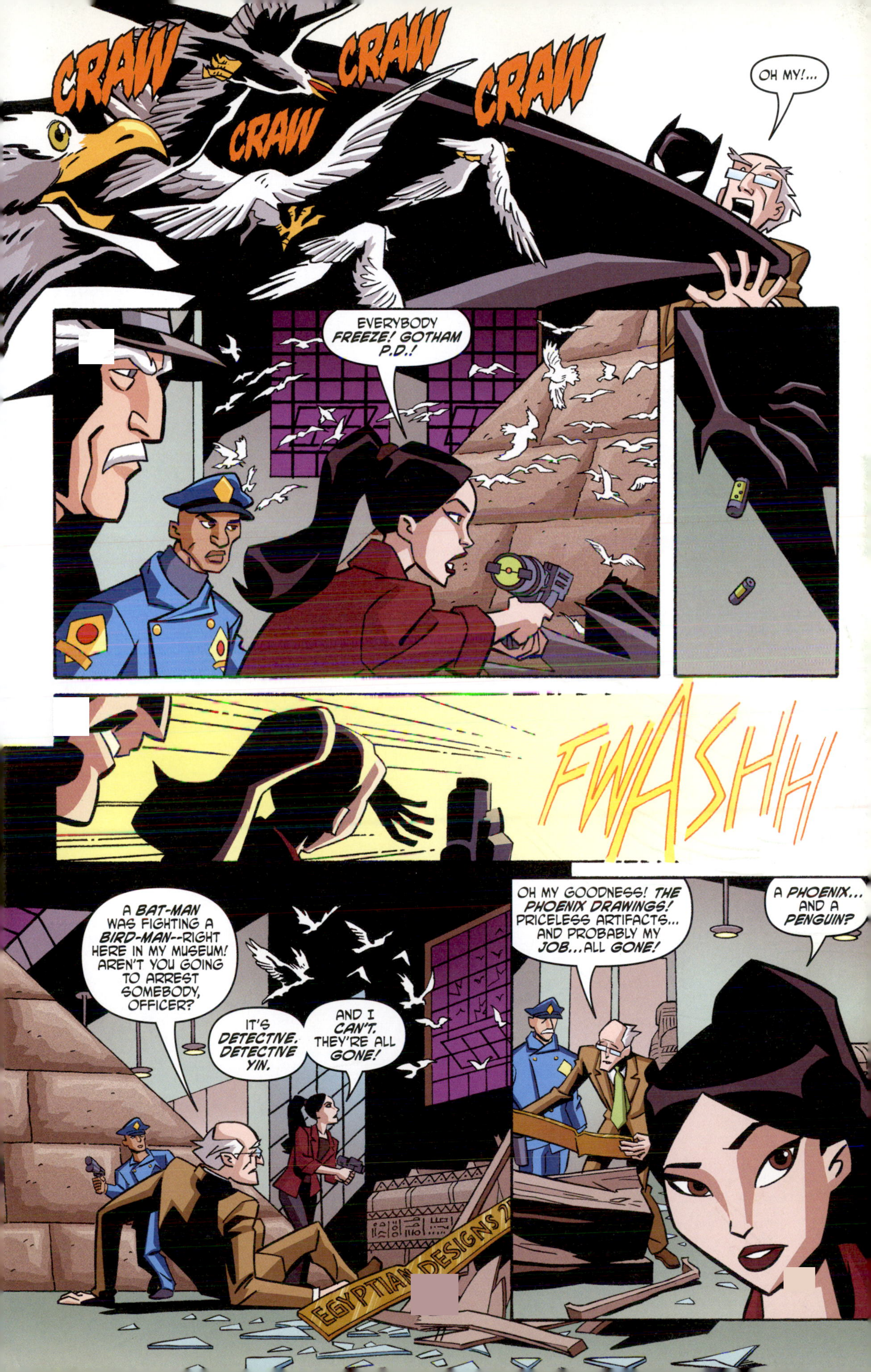
CRAW
CRAW
CRAW
CRAW
OH MY!...
EVERYBODY FREEZE! GOTHAM P.D.!
FWASHH
A BAT-MAN WAS FIGHTING A BIRD-MAN--RIGHT HERE IN MY MUSEUM! AREN'T YOU GOING TO ARREST SOMEBODY, OFFICER?
IT'S DETECTIVE. DETECTIVE YIN.
AND I CAN'T. THEY'RE ALL GONE!
EGYPTIAN DESIGNS
OH MY GOODNESS! THE PHOENIX DRAWINGS! PRICELESS ARTIFACTS... AND PROBABLY MY JOB...ALL GONE!
A PHOENIX... AND A PENGUIN?

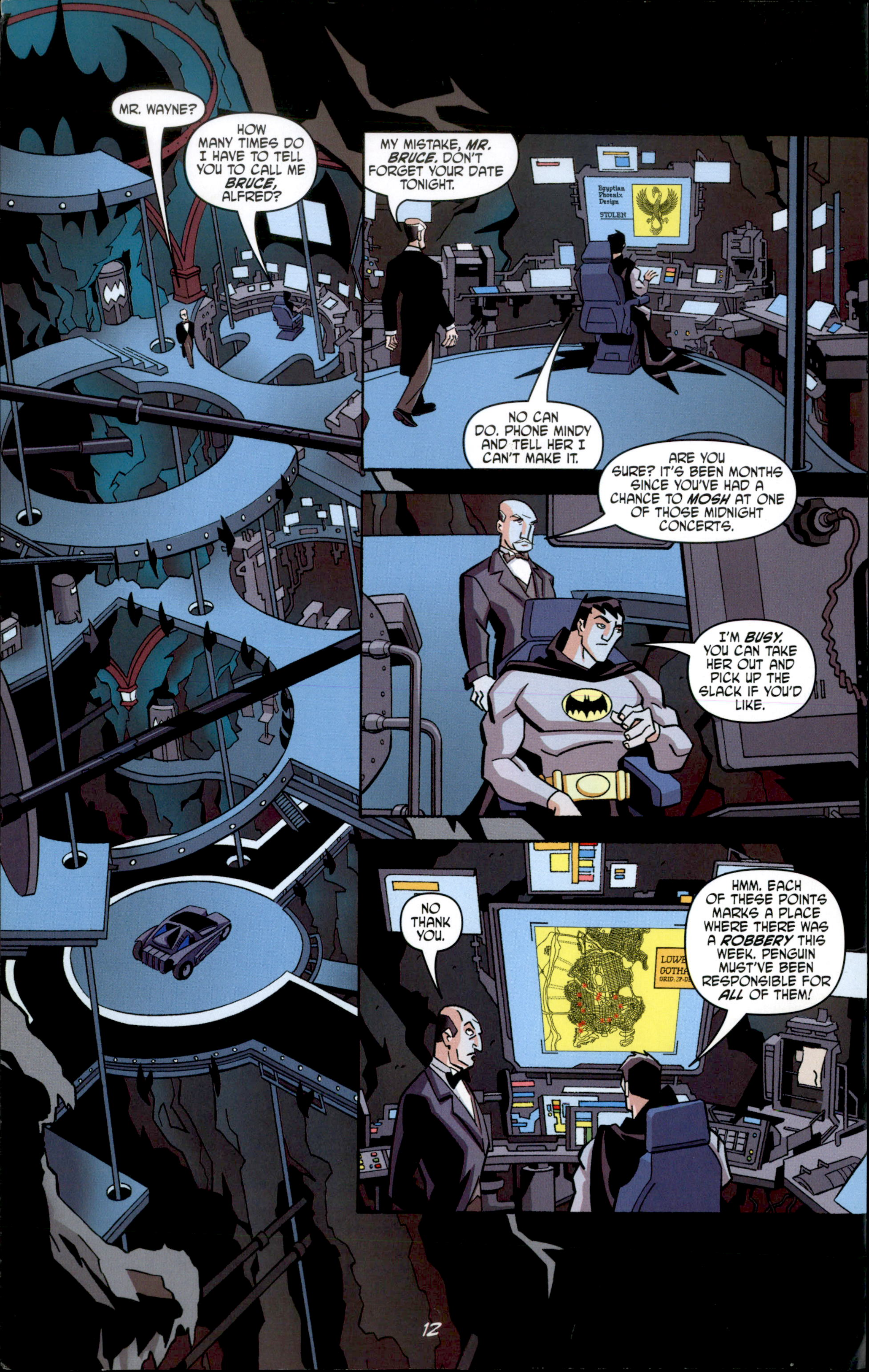

MR. WAYNE?
HOW MANY TIMES DO I HAVE TO TELL YOU TO CALL ME BRUCE, ALFRED?
MY MISTAKE, MR. BRUCE. DON'T FORGET YOUR DATE TONIGHT.
Egyptian Phoenix Design
STOLEN
NO CAN DO. PHONE MINDY AND TELL HER I CAN'T MAKE IT.
ARE YOU SURE? IT'S BEEN MONTHS SINCE YOU'VE HAD A CHANCE TO MOSH AT ONE OF THOSE MIDNIGHT CONCERTS.
I'M BUSY. YOU CAN TAKE HER OUT AND PICK UP THE SLACK IF YOU'D LIKE.
NO THANK YOU.
HMM. EACH OF THESE POINTS MARKS A PLACE WHERE THERE WAS A ROBBERY THIS WEEK. PENGUIN MUST'VE BEEN RESPONSIBLE FOR ALL OF THEM!

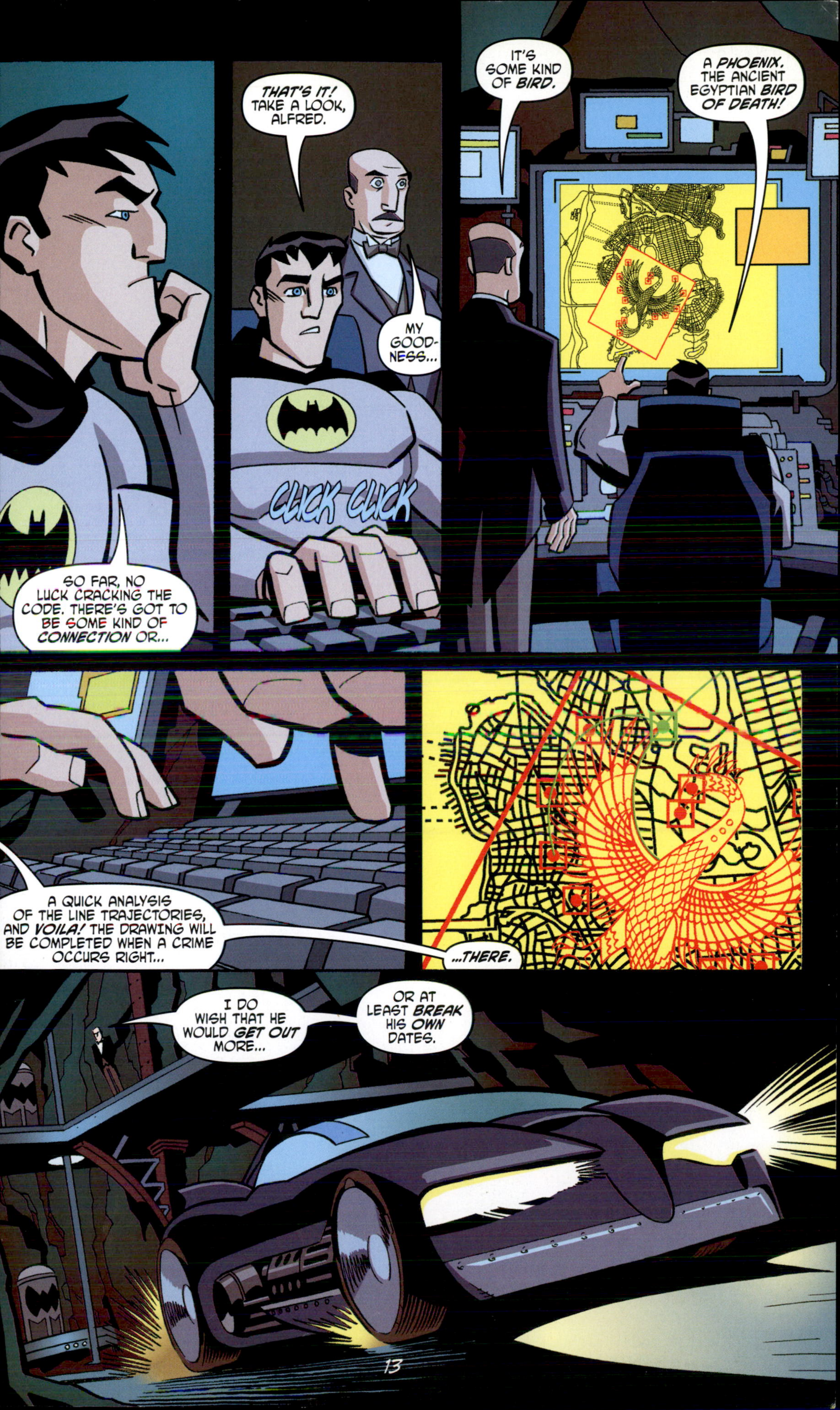
SO FAR, NO LUCK CRACKING THE CODE. THERE'S GOT TO BE SOME KIND OF CONNECTION OR...
THAT'S IT! TAKE A LOOK, ALFRED.
CLICK CLICK
MY GOODNESS...
IT'S SOME KIND OF BIRD.
A PHOENIX. THE ANCIENT EGYPTIAN BIRD OF DEATH!
A QUICK ANALYSIS OF THE LINE TRAJECTORIES, AND VOILA! THE DRAWING WILL BE COMPLETED WHEN A CRIME OCCURS RIGHT...
...THERE.
I DO WISH THAT HE WOULD GET OUT MORE...
OR AT LEAST BREAK HIS OWN DATES.

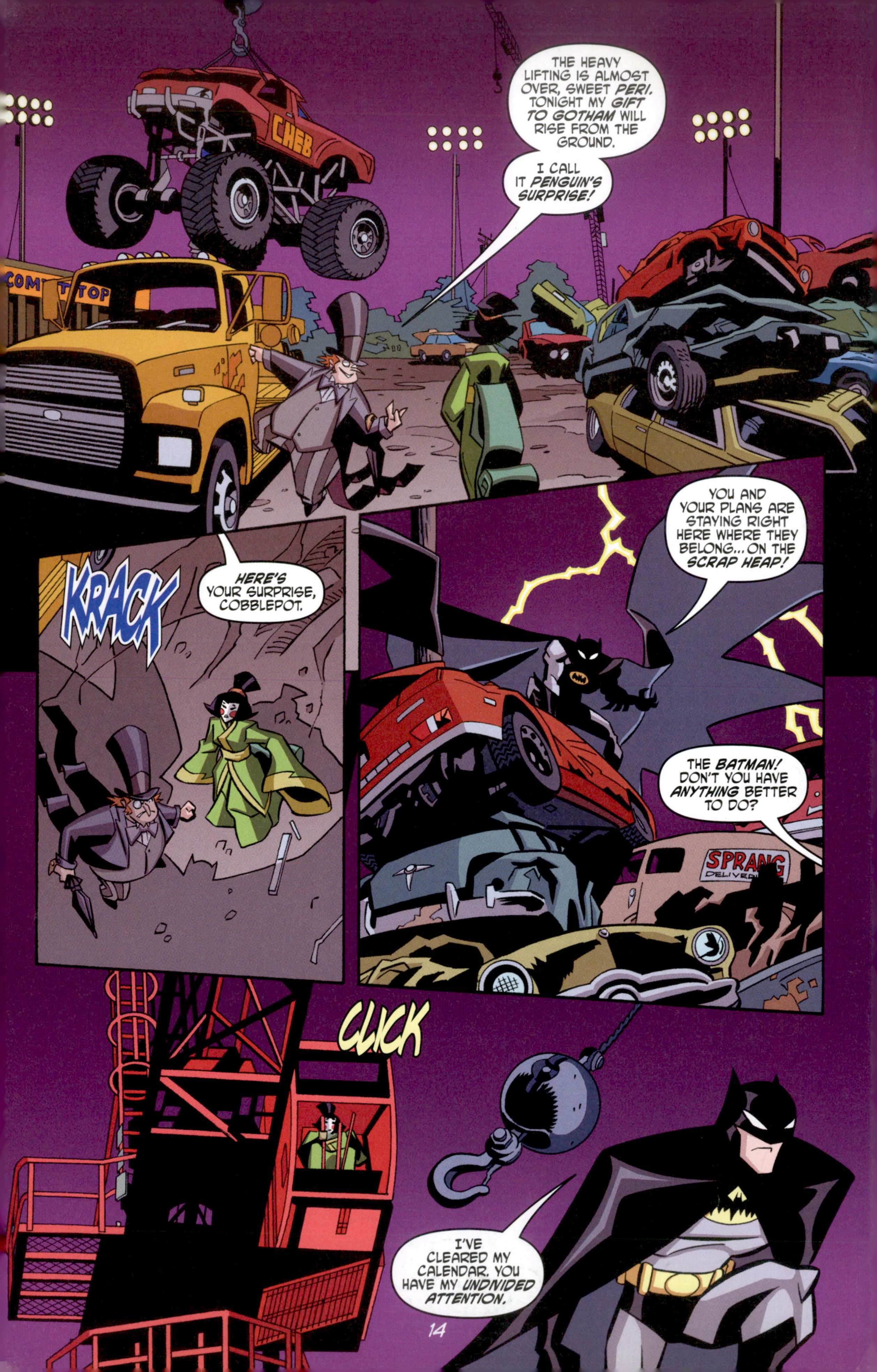
THE HEAVY LIFTING IS ALMOST OVER, SWEET PERI. TONIGHT MY GIFT TO GOTHAM WILL RISE FROM THE GROUND.
I CALL IT PENGUIN'S SURPRISE!
CHEB
KRACK
HERE'S YOUR SURPRISE, COBBLEPOT.
YOU AND YOUR PLANS ARE STAYING RIGHT HERE WHERE THEY BELONG... ON THE SCRAP HEAP!
THE BATMAN! DON'T YOU HAVE ANYTHING BETTER TO DO?
SPRANG
CLICK
I'VE CLEARED MY CALENDAR. YOU HAVE MY UNDIVIDED ATTENTION.

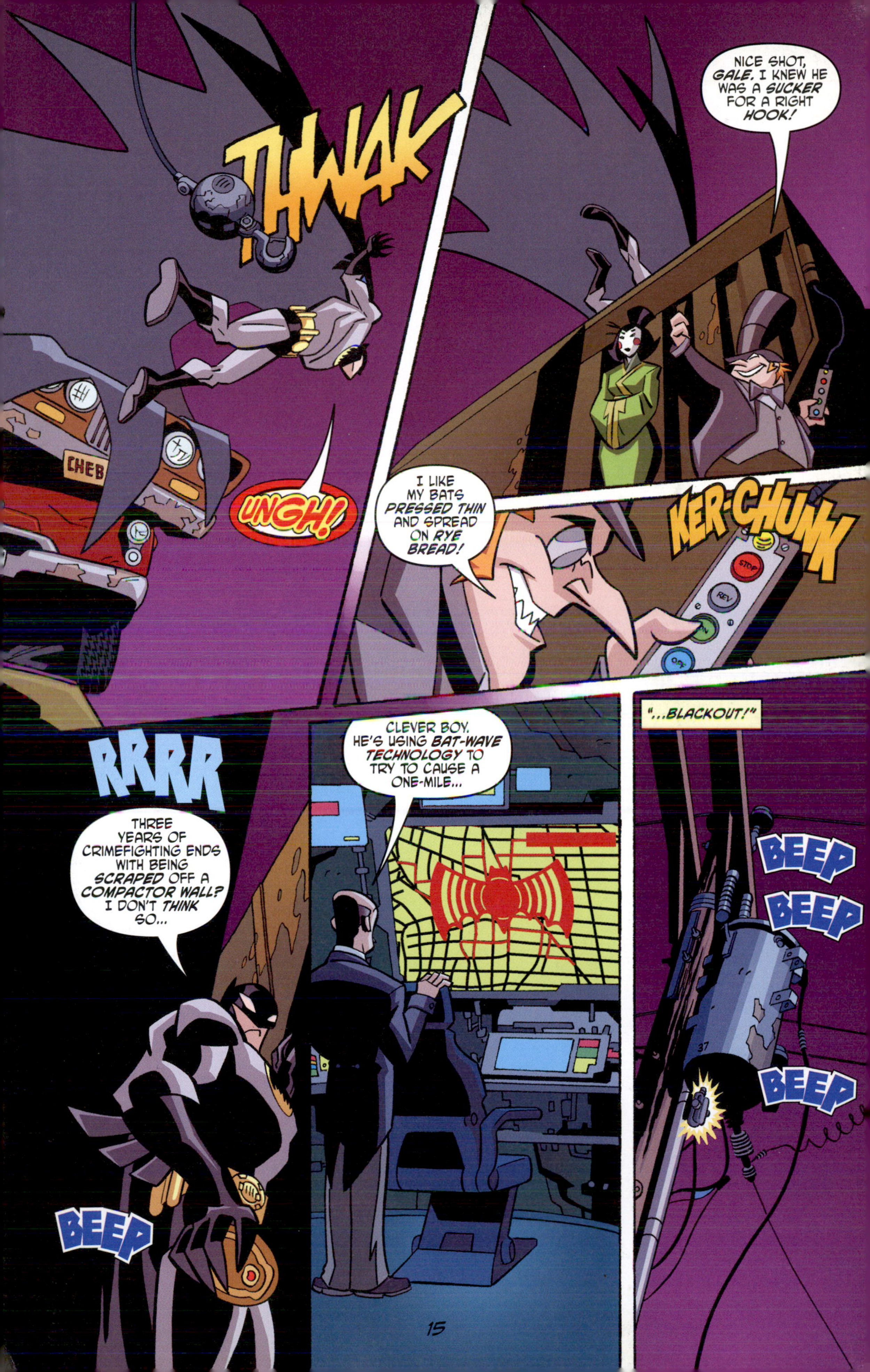
THWAK
UNGH!
NICE SHOT, GALE. I KNEW HE WAS A SUCKER FOR A RIGHT HOOK!
I LIKE MY BATS PRESSED THIN AND SPREAD ON RYE BREAD!
KER-CHUNK
RRRR
THREE YEARS OF CRIMEFIGHTING ENDS WITH BEING SCRAPED OFF A COMPACTOR WALL? I DON'T THINK SO...
BEEP
CLEVER BOY. HE'S USING BAT-WAVE TECHNOLOGY TO TRY TO CAUSE A ONE-MILE...
"...BLACKOUT!"
BEEP
BEEP
BEEP

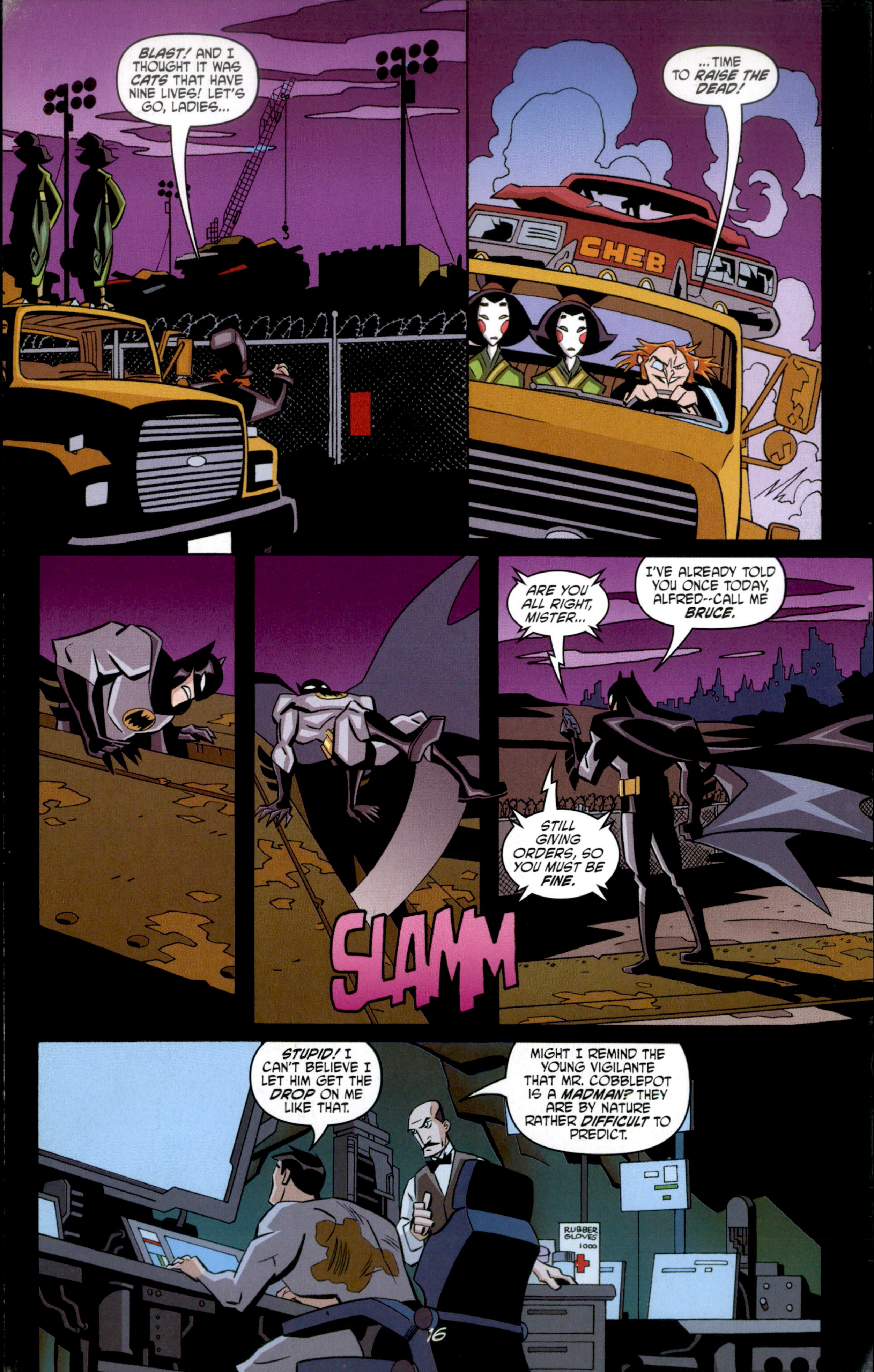

BLAST! AND I THOUGHT IT WAS CATS THAT HAVE NINE LIVES! LET'S GO, LADIES...
...TIME TO RAISE THE DEAD!
CHEB
ARE YOU ALL RIGHT, MISTER...
I'VE ALREADY TOLD YOU ONCE TODAY, ALFRED--CALL ME BRUCE.
STILL GIVING ORDERS, SO YOU MUST BE FINE.
SLAMM
STUPID! I CAN'T BELIEVE I LET HIM GET THE DROP ON ME LIKE THAT.
MIGHT I REMIND THE YOUNG VIGILANTE THAT MR. COBBLEPOT IS A MADMAN? THEY ARE BY NATURE RATHER DIFFICULT TO PREDICT.
RUBBER GLOVES 1000

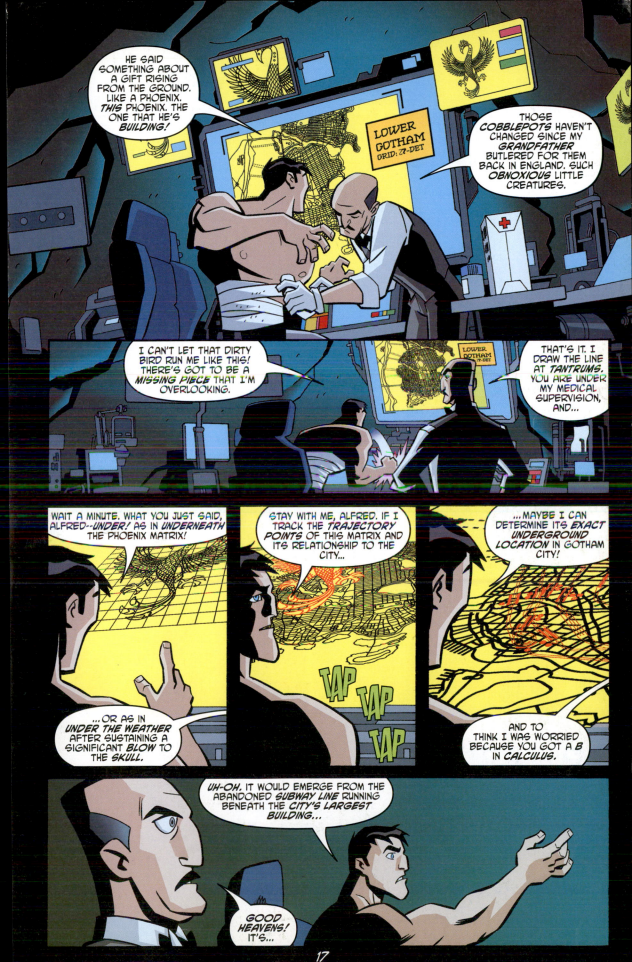

HE SAID SOMETHING ABOUT A GIFT RISING FROM THE GROUND. LIKE A PHOENIX. *THIS* PHOENIX. THE ONE THAT HE'S *BUILDING!*

LOWER GOTHAM GRID: 77-DET

THOSE *COBBLEPOTS* HAVEN'T CHANGED SINCE MY *GRANDFATHER* BUTLERED FOR THEM BACK IN ENGLAND. SUCH *OBNOXIOUS* LITTLE CREATURES.

I CAN'T LET THAT DIRTY BIRD RUN ME LIKE THIS! THERE'S GOT TO BE A *MISSING PIECE* THAT I'M OVERLOOKING.

THAT'S IT. I DRAW THE LINE AT *TANTRUMS.* YOU ARE UNDER MY MEDICAL SUPERVISION, AND...

WAIT A MINUTE. WHAT YOU JUST SAID, ALFRED--*UNDER!* AS IN *UNDERNEATH* THE PHOENIX MATRIX!

...OR AS IN *UNDER THE WEATHER* AFTER SUSTAINING A SIGNIFICANT *BLOW* TO THE *SKULL.*

STAY WITH ME, ALFRED. IF I TRACK THE *TRAJECTORY POINTS* OF THIS MATRIX AND ITS RELATIONSHIP TO THE CITY...

TAP TAP TAP

...MAYBE I CAN DETERMINE ITS *EXACT UNDERGROUND LOCATION* IN GOTHAM CITY!

AND TO THINK I WAS WORRIED BECAUSE YOU GOT A *B* IN *CALCULUS.*

UH-OH. IT WOULD EMERGE FROM THE ABANDONED *SUBWAY LINE* RUNNING BENEATH THE *CITY'S LARGEST BUILDING...*

GOOD HEAVENS! IT'S...

17

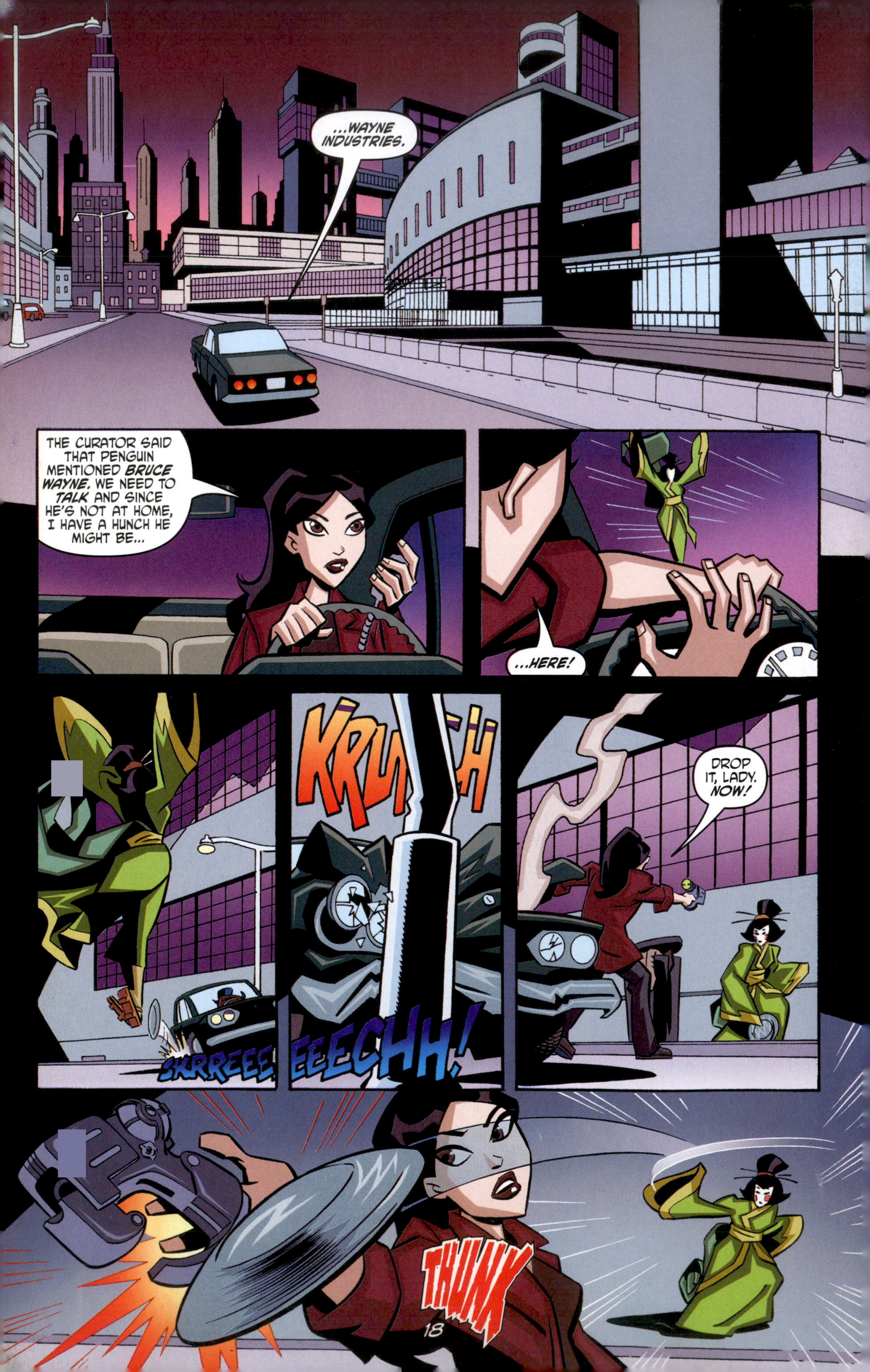
...WAYNE INDUSTRIES.
THE CURATOR SAID THAT PENGUIN MENTIONED BRUCE WAYNE. WE NEED TO TALK AND SINCE HE'S NOT AT HOME, I HAVE A HUNCH HE MIGHT BE...
...HERE!
KRUNCH
SKRREEEEEECHH!
DROP IT, LADY. NOW!
THUNK
18

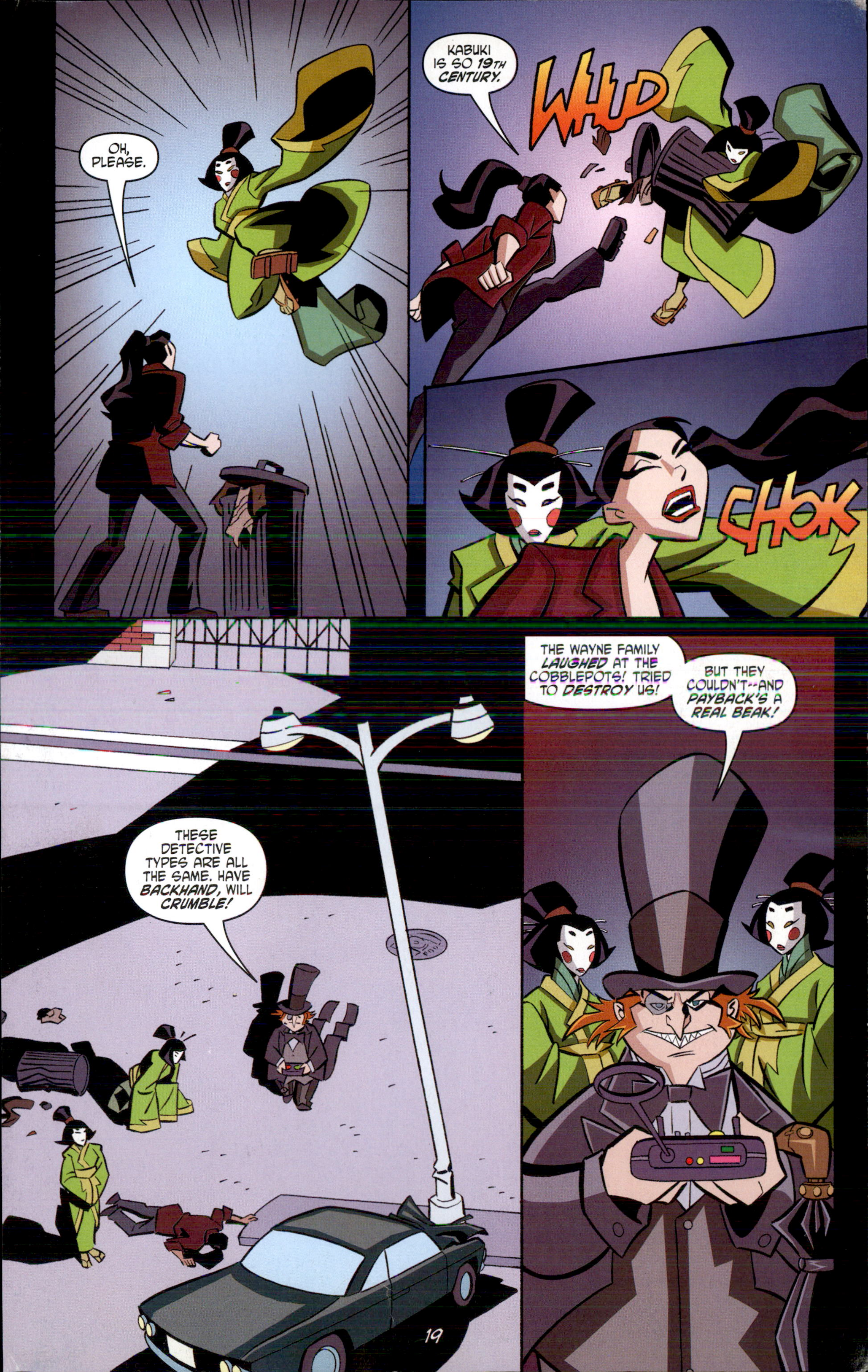
OH, PLEASE.
KABUKI IS SO 19TH CENTURY.
WHUD
CHOK
THESE DETECTIVE TYPES ARE ALL THE SAME. HAVE BACKHAND, WILL CRUMBLE!
THE WAYNE FAMILY LAUGHED AT THE COBBLEPOTS! TRIED TO DESTROY US!
BUT THEY COULDN'T--AND PAYBACK'S A REAL BEAK!

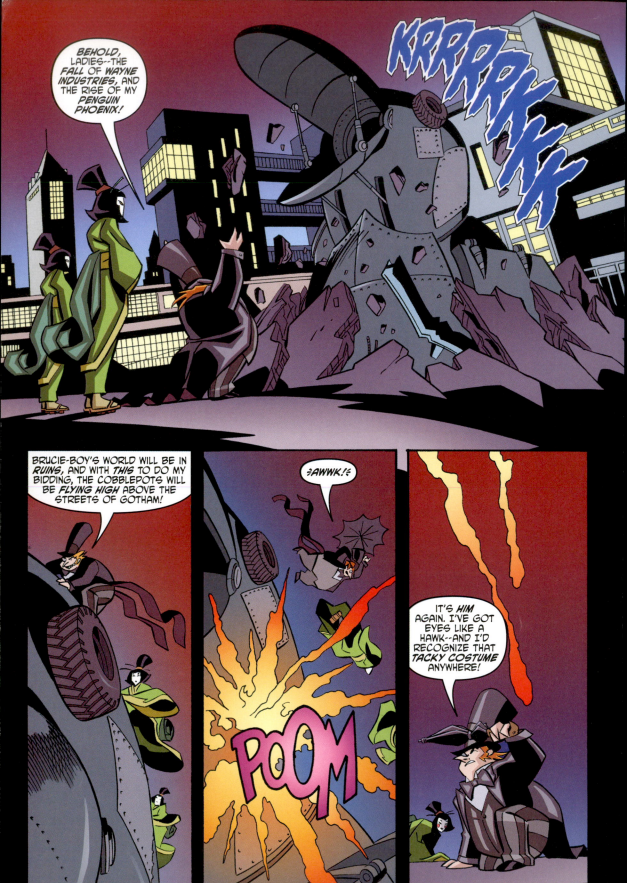

BEHOLD, LADIES--THE *FALL OF WAYNE INDUSTRIES,* AND THE RISE OF MY *PENGUIN PHOENIX!*

KRRRRKKK

BRUCIE-BOY'S WORLD WILL BE IN *RUINS,* AND WITH *THIS* TO DO MY BIDDING, THE COBBLEPOTS WILL BE *FLYING HIGH* ABOVE THE STREETS OF GOTHAM!

≨AWWK!≩

POOM

IT'S *HIM* AGAIN. I'VE GOT EYES LIKE A HAWK--AND I'D RECOGNIZE THAT *TACKY COSTUME* ANYWHERE!

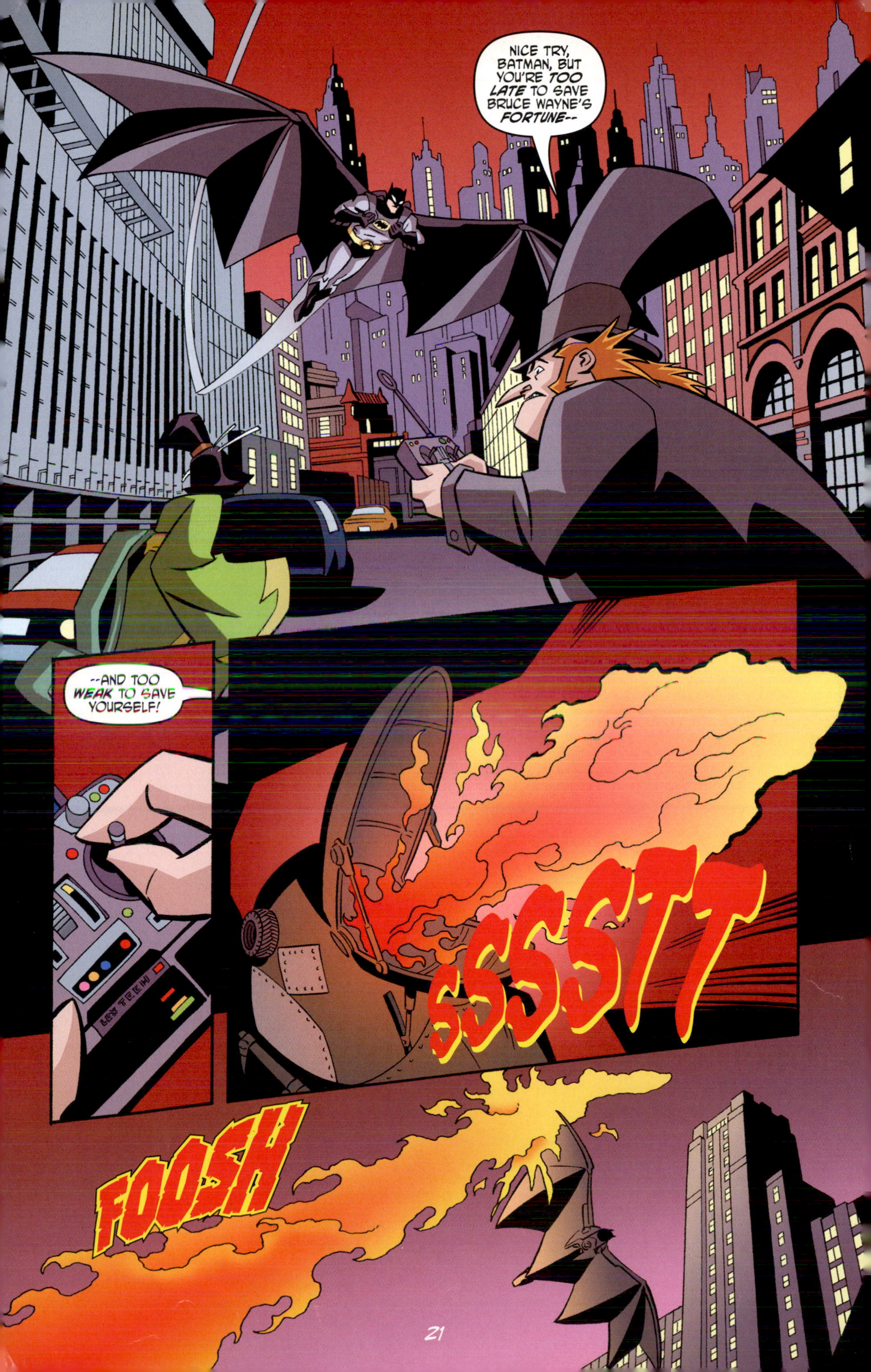
NICE TRY, BATMAN, BUT YOU'RE TOO LATE TO SAVE BRUCE WAYNE'S FORTUNE--
--AND TOO WEAK TO SAVE YOURSELF!
LEX TECH
SSSSTT
FOOSH

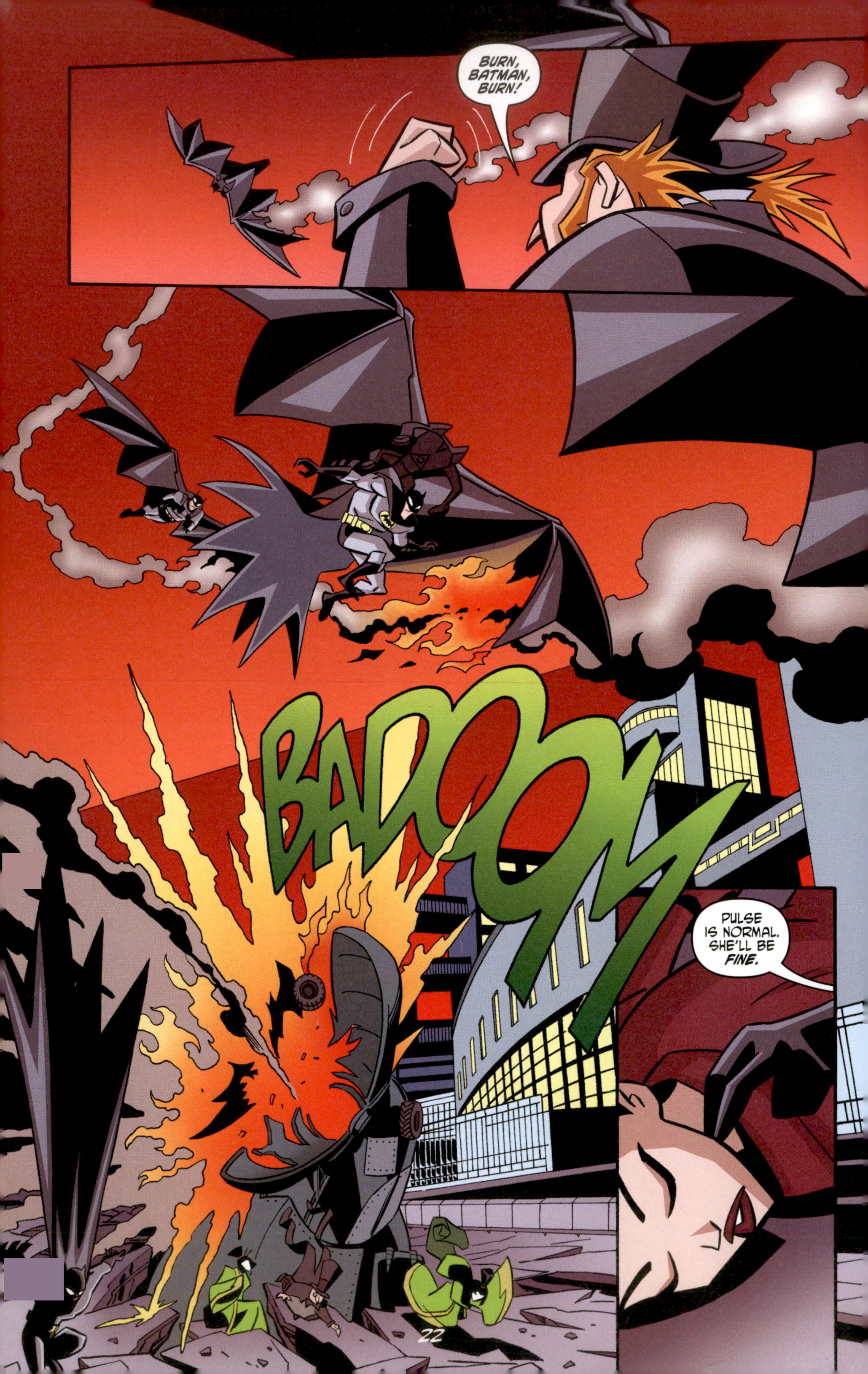
BURN, BATMAN, BURN!
BADOOM
PULSE IS NORMAL. SHE'LL BE FINE.

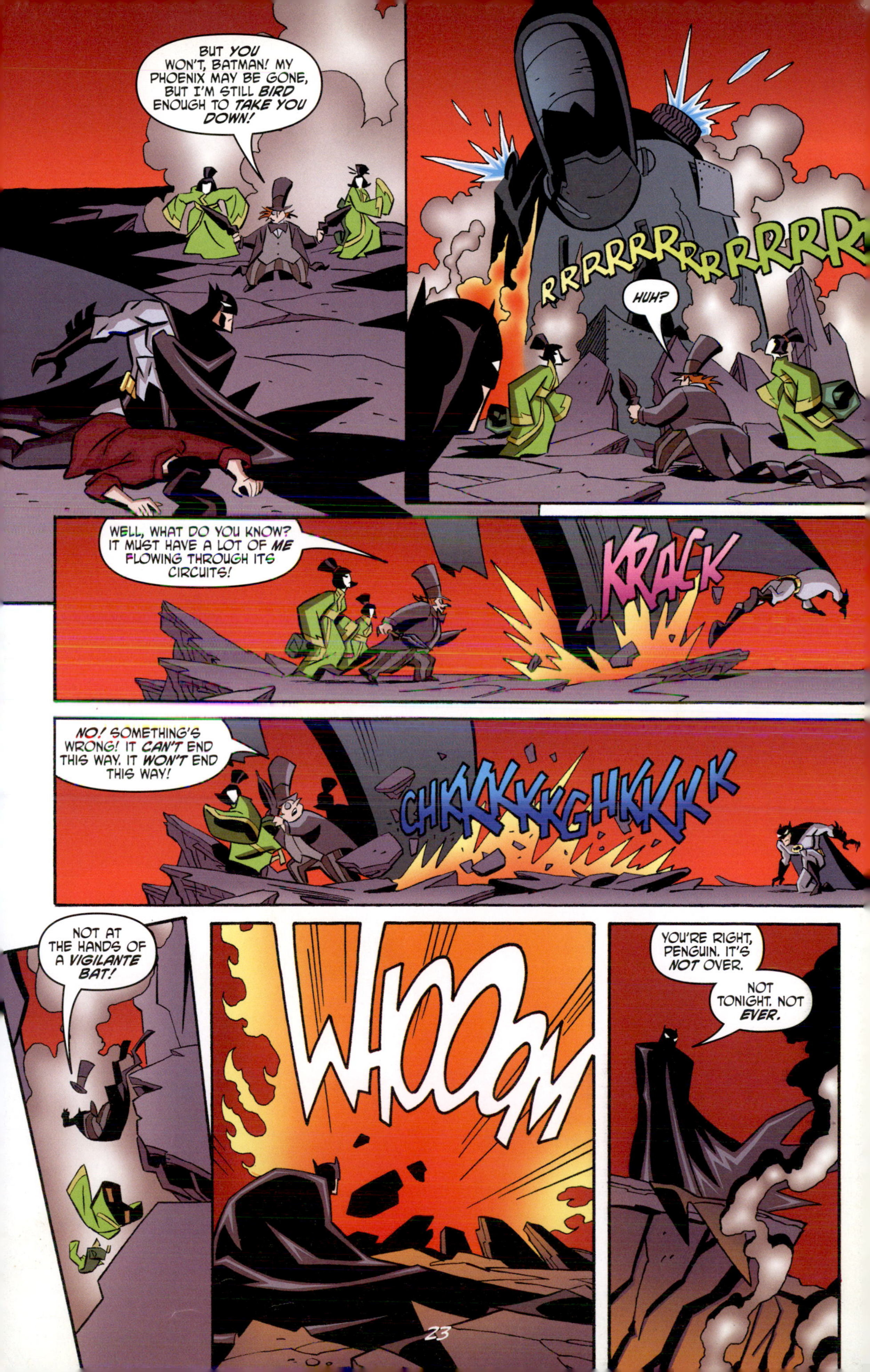
BUT YOU WON'T, BATMAN! MY PHOENIX MAY BE GONE, BUT I'M STILL BIRD ENOUGH TO TAKE YOU DOWN!
RRRRRRRRRRRRRR
HUH?
WELL, WHAT DO YOU KNOW? IT MUST HAVE A LOT OF ME FLOWING THROUGH ITS CIRCUITS!
KRACK
NO! SOMETHING'S WRONG! IT CAN'T END THIS WAY. IT WON'T END THIS WAY!
CHKKKKKGHKKKKK
NOT AT THE HANDS OF A VIGILANTE BAT!
WHOOM
YOU'RE RIGHT, PENGUIN. IT'S NOT OVER.
NOT TONIGHT. NOT EVER.

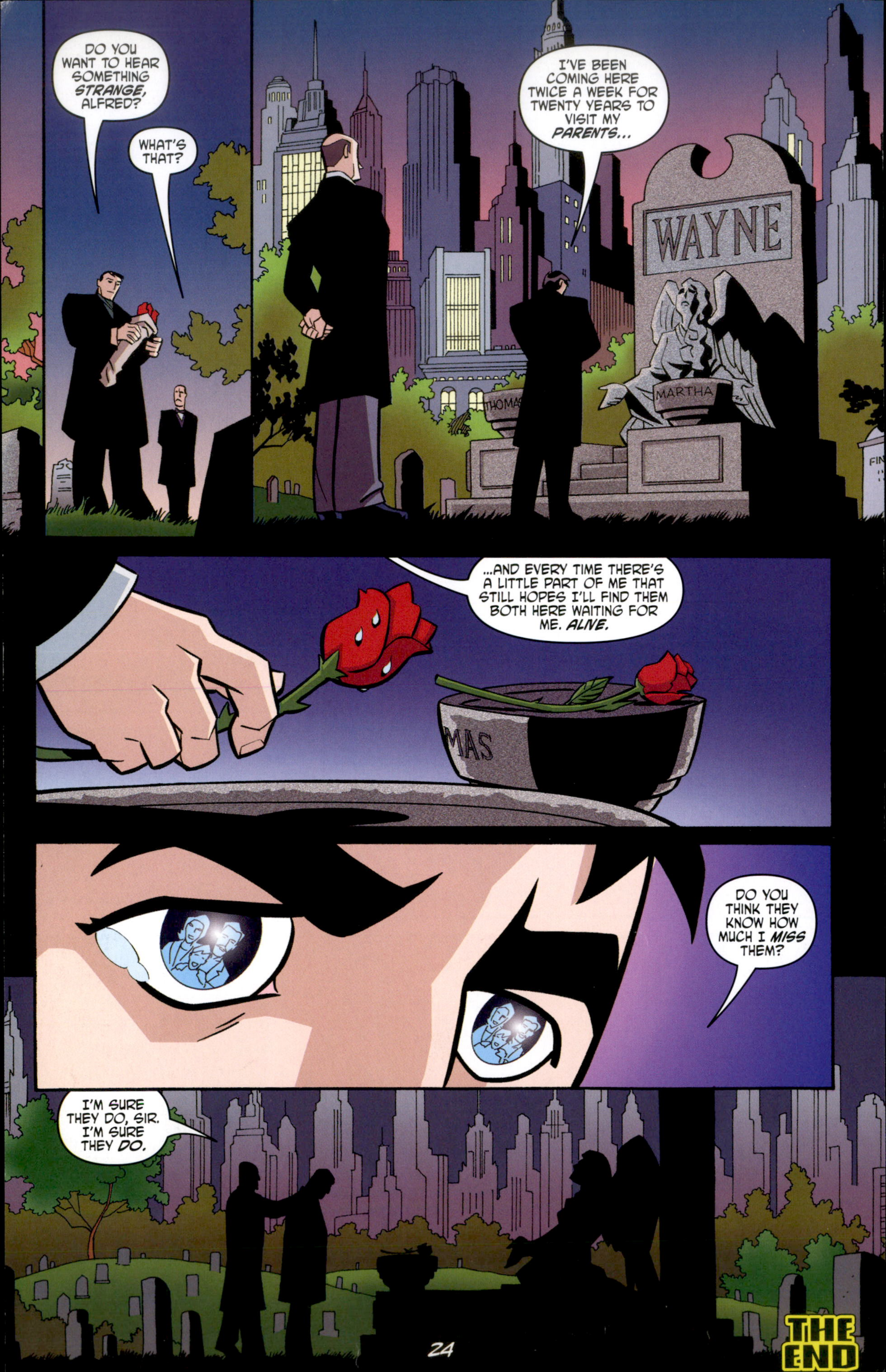
DO YOU WANT TO HEAR SOMETHING STRANGE, ALFRED?
WHAT'S THAT?
I'VE BEEN COMING HERE TWICE A WEEK FOR TWENTY YEARS TO VISIT MY PARENTS...
WAYNE
THOMAS
MARTHA
...AND EVERY TIME THERE'S A LITTLE PART OF ME THAT STILL HOPES I'LL FIND THEM BOTH HERE WAITING FOR ME. ALIVE.
MAS
DO YOU THINK THEY KNOW HOW MUCH I MISS THEM?
I'M SURE THEY DO, SIR. I'M SURE THEY DO.
THE END

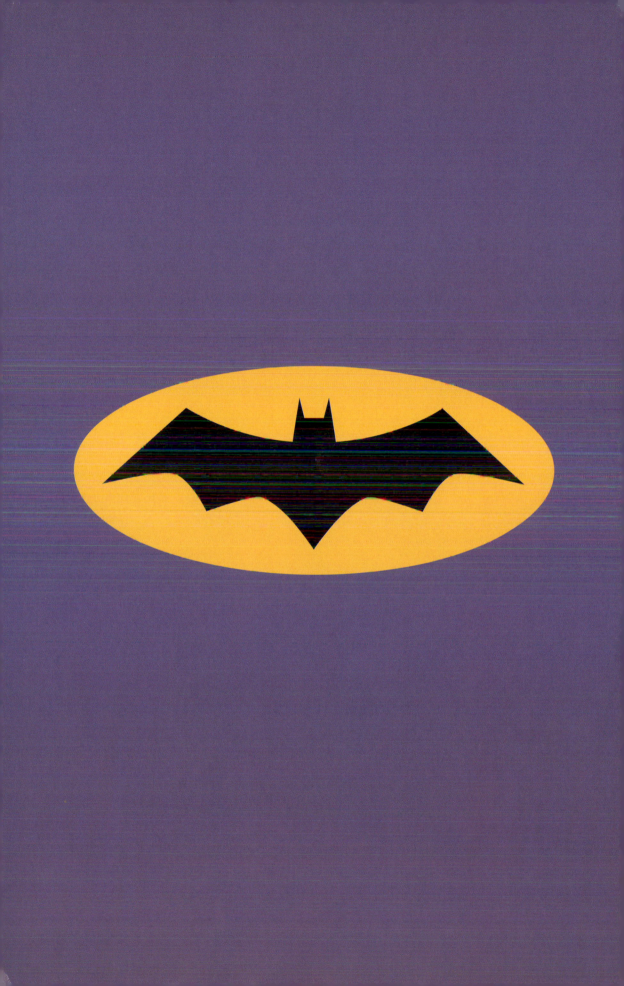

CREATORS

BILL MATHENY WRITER

Along with comics like THE BATMAN STRIKES, Bill Matheny has written for TV series including KRYPTO THE SUPERDOG, WHERE'S WALDO, A PUP NAMED SCOOBY-DOO, and many others.

CHRISTOPHER JONES PENCILLER

Christopher Jones is an artist that has worked for DC Comics, Image, Malibu, Caliber, and Sundragon Comics.

TERRY BEATTY INKER

Terry Beatty has inked THE BATMAN STRIKES! and BATMAN: THE BRAVE AND THE BOLD as well as several other DC Comics graphic novels.

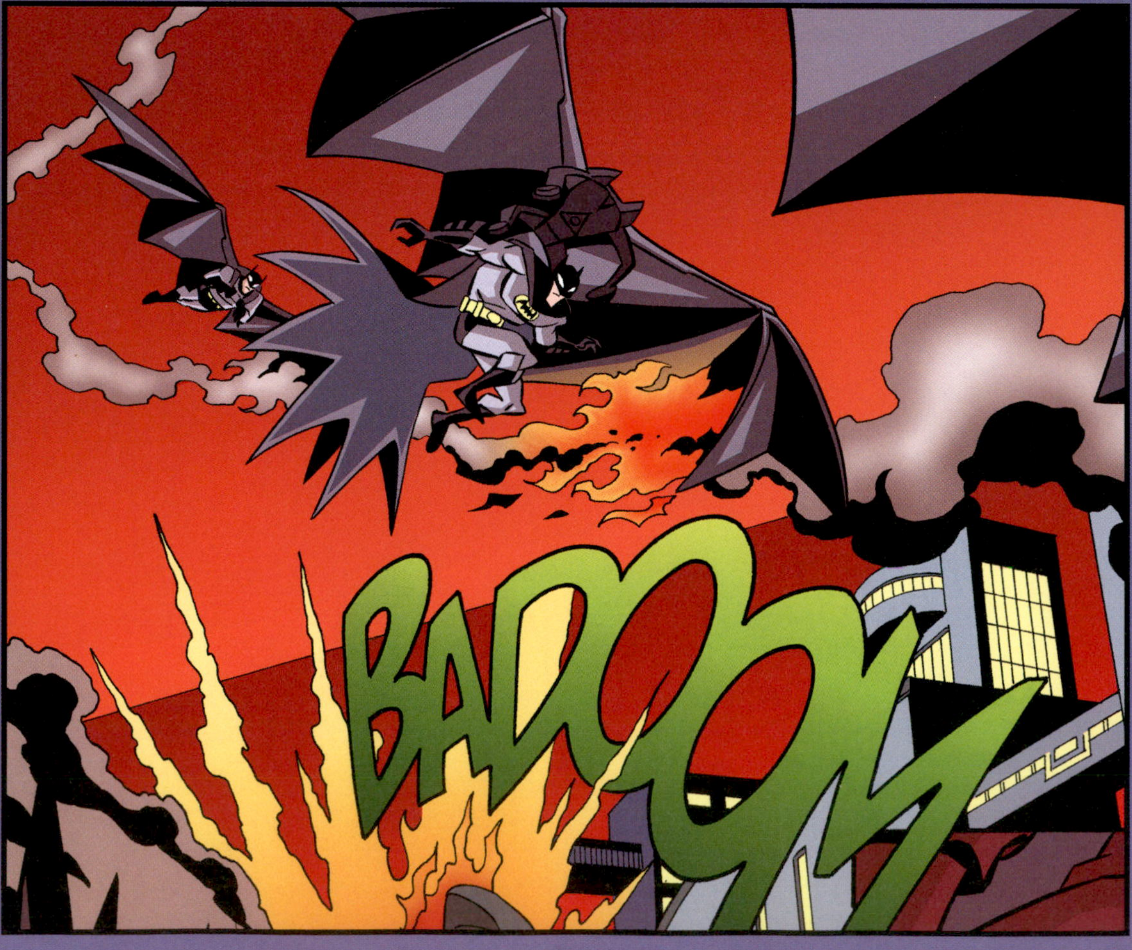
BADOOOM

GLOSSARY

acknowledging (ak-NOL-uh-jing)-- greeting someone

analysis (uh-NAL-uh-sis)--the process of studying something very closely

artifacts (ART-uh-faktz)--objects from the past that were made or changed by human beings

curator (KYOO-ray-tur)--the person in charge of a museum or art gallery

dedicated (DED-uh-kay-tid)--gave a lot of energy and time to something or someone

kabuki (kuh-BOO-kee)--a type of Japanese drama traditionally performed by men in elaborate costumes

oaf (OAF)--fool

obnoxious (uhb-NOK-shuhss)--very unpleasant, annoying, or offensive

tacky (TAK-ee)--cheap or corny

trajectories (truh-JEK-tor-eez)--arcs that objects travel

vigilante (vij-uh-LAN-tee)--someone who takes the law into their own hands

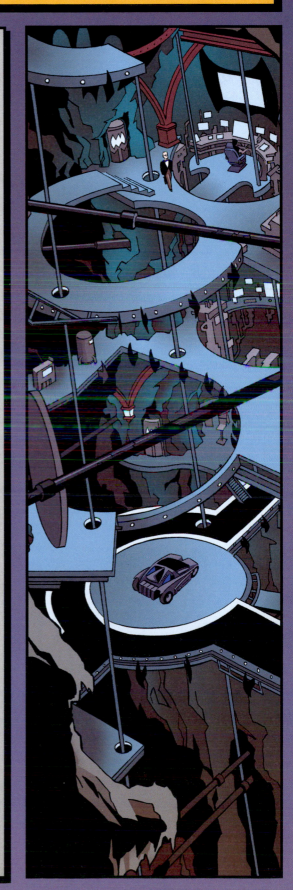

VISUAL QUESTIONS & PROMPTS

1. Batman uses many tools to fight crime. Here he uses a batarang attached to a rope to grab hold of the Penguin. Design a new tool for Batman. What does it do? How does it work?

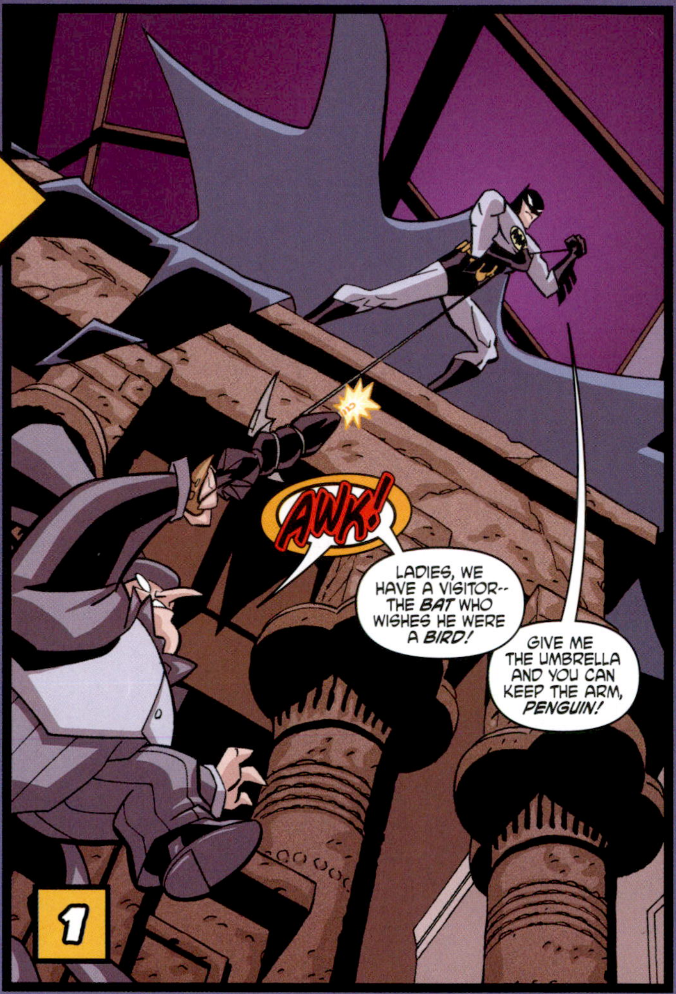
AWK!
LADIES, WE HAVE A VISITOR-- THE *BAT* WHO WISHES HE WERE A *BIRD!*
GIVE ME THE UMBRELLA AND YOU CAN KEEP THE ARM, *PENGUIN!*
1

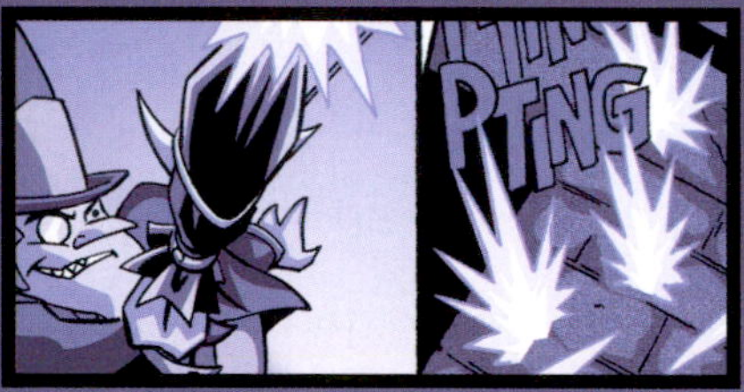
PTING

2. Based on these two panels, what do you think the bat-wave technology does? Explain your answer using examples from the book.

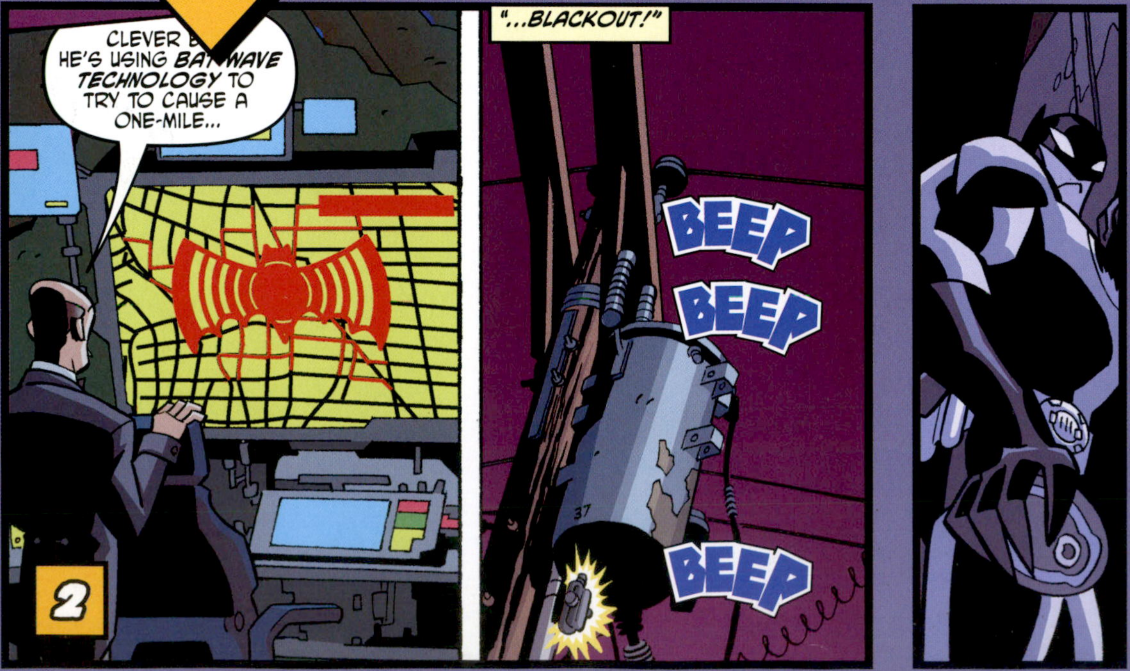
CLEVER
HE'S USING TECHNOLOGY TO TRY TO CAUSE A ONE-MILE...
"...BLACKOUT!"
BEEP
BEEP
BEEP
2

3. Batman's symbol represents his super hero identity. Create your own super hero symbol. Is it based on an animal or something else? What would you choose for your super hero name?

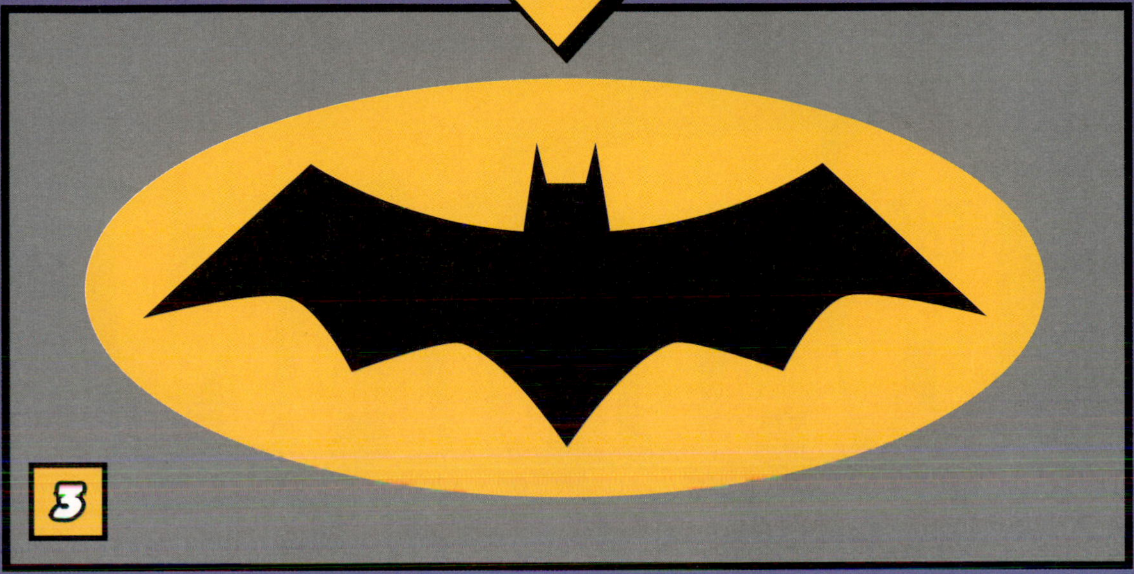
3

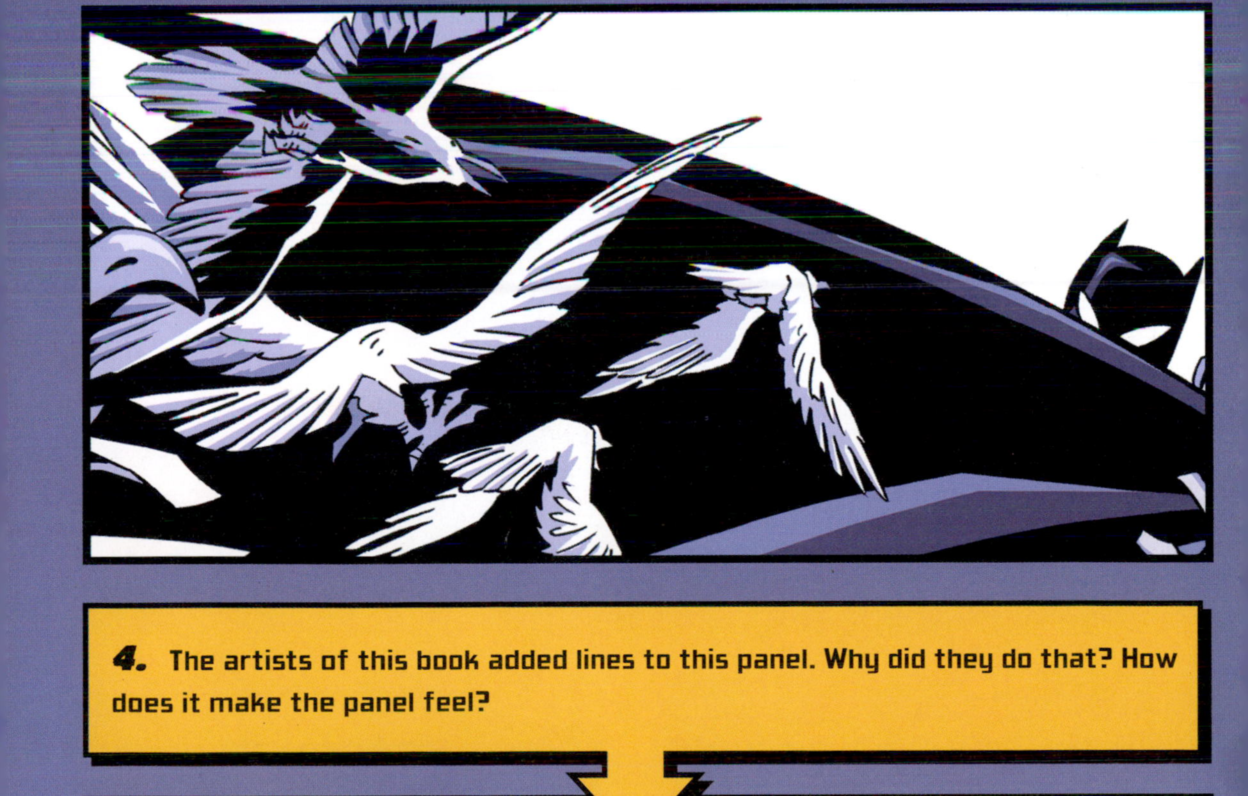

4. The artists of this book added lines to this panel. Why did they do that? How does it make the panel feel?

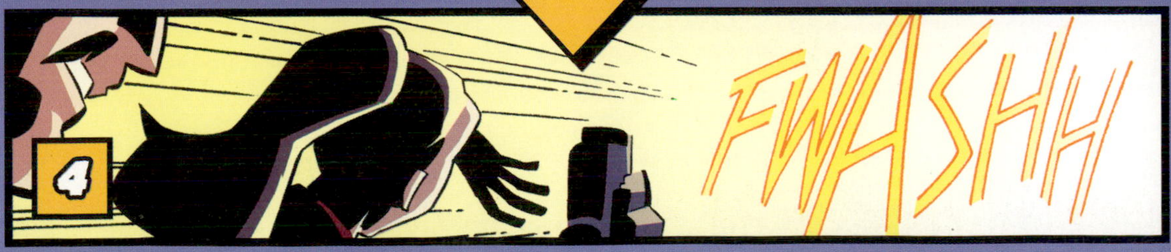
4
FWASHH

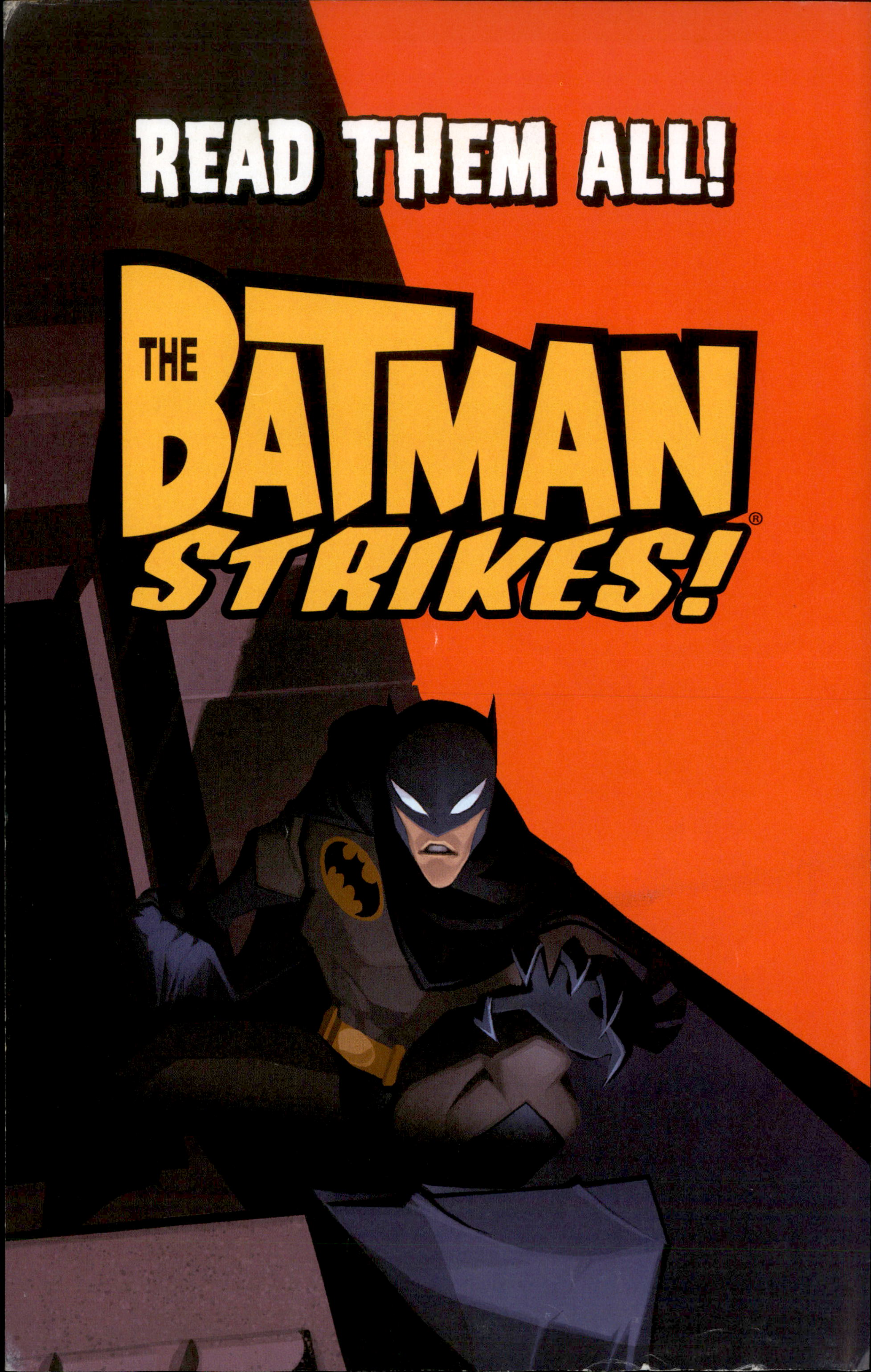
READ THEM ALL!
THE BATMAN STRIKES!

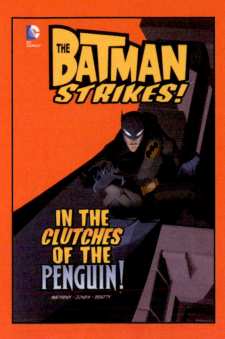

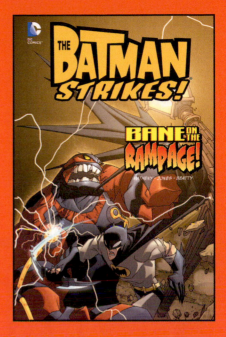

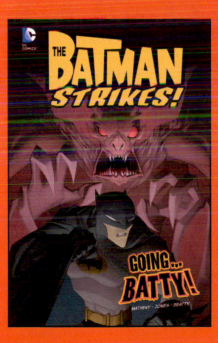

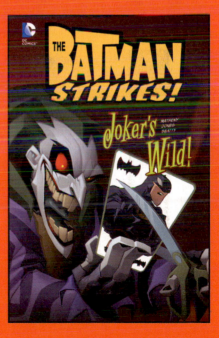

THE BATMAN STRIKES!
IN THE CLUTCHES OF THE PENGUIN!
MATHENY · JONES · BEATTY

THE BATMAN STRIKES!
BANE ON THE RAMPAGE!
MATHENY · JONES · BEATTY

THE BATMAN STRIKES!
GOING... BATTY!
MATHENY · JONES · BEATTY

THE BATMAN STRIKES!
Joker's Wild!
MATHENY
JONES
BEATTY

THE BATMAN STRIKES!®

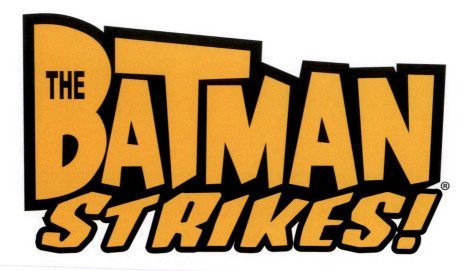